The STOWAWAY

Hippolyte de Bouchard

Courtesy of The Colton Hall Museum
City of Monterey
Monterey, CA

The STOWAWAY

A Tale of California Pirates

KRISTIANA GREGORY

SCHOLASTIC INC.
New York Toronto London Auckland Sydney
Mexico City New Delhi Hong Kong Buenos Aires

ISBN-13: 978-0-590-48823-5
ISBN-10: 0-590-48823-6

30 29 28 27 26 25 24 23 22 10 11 12/0

Printed in the U.S.A. 40

First paperback printing, December 1997

With love to my wonderful nieces and nephews:
Billy, Brett, Cari Lynn, Dusty, Hailey,
Joey, Kevin, Lauren, Matthew, Nic,
Pente, Scott, Scotty, and Woodrow.

Acknowledgments

Julian Hudson Blakeley, for the use of his extensive library on California history; my brother Rob Gregory, for reminiscences about life at sea and aboard a three-masted barkentine, and for Spanish translations; my father Hal Gregory, for his pirate books and nautical expertise; my ever-helpful friends at A.K. Smiley Library and Heritage Room in Redlands, CA; Hilda Viskovic, for checking the Spanish terms; Heather Saunders, for drawing the maps; the captain and crew aboard the brig *Pilgrim* at Orange County Marine Institute in Dana Point, CA; and the Monterey Peninsula Chamber of Commerce.

Contents

Contenido

Note

Nota

The Stowaway: A Tale of California Pirates is historical fiction based on the true exploits of Hippolyte de Bouchard, captain of the 42-gun frigate *Argentina*.

Born in 1783 in St. Tropez, France, Bouchard moved to Buenos Aires, Argentina, as a young man, married a local girl, and served in the Argentine navy during the country's struggle for independence from Spain. As a privateer authorized to attack and capture enemy ships in the name of the Argentine government, he began an around-the-world voyage on July 9, 1817.

After rounding Africa's Cape of Good Hope, he sailed to Madagascar, Indonesia, and the Philippines, raiding Spanish ships and ports along the way. When his decks became too heavy with treasure, he sought harbor in the Sandwich Islands (Hawaii) to unload as well as to find new crew members. Nearly 100 men died of scurvy during twelve months at sea.

While anchored in Honolulu, Bouchard noticed the

Santa Rosa, a corvette whose crew had mutinied after a harrowing voyage around Cape Horn. The little ship was now owned by King Kamehameha, who had confiscated it and its cargo. Because the *Santa Rosa* was also from Buenos Aires, Bouchard tricked the king into turning it over to him, then hired Peter Corney to be its commander. Corney, a chief officer with the British schooner *Columbia*, had been relaxing in Honolulu. He was flattered that Bouchard wanted him and he was eager to captain his own vessel.

Together, the two ships searched among the islands for the *Santa Rosa*'s mutineers, partly to bring them aboard as sailors, but also to punish the leaders. Bouchard, whose brutality and violent temper terrified even the roughest pirate, soon found some of the men on the island of Kauai. First Lieutenant Griffiths was dragged from the jungle to the beach, blindfolded, then shot by four marines. With the Argentine flag flying, hundreds of natives witnessed his execution and quick burial at high-water mark. Other mutineers were found on the island of Maui and flogged until their backs split open.

Bouchard's next plan was to attack Monterey and the Spanish missions of Alta (upper) California. The two ships returned from Kauai to Oahu for vegetables, fruits, hogs, and water. Eighty Sandwich Islanders joined the crews, which were an unsavory mix of cutthroats and thieves from around the world: Americans, Spaniards, Australians, Portuguese, Africans, Malaysians, and Englishmen.

Finally on October 20, 1818, the *Argentina* and *Santa Rosa* left the islands. During the passage to California the pirates practiced shooting their cannons. Frequently came the order "All hands on deck!" While the men stood at attention, an officer read aloud the Articles of War, which were the navy's strict laws. Bouchard emphasized that any sailor or soldier who disobeyed orders could be punished with death.

Meanwhile a certain Captain Gyzelaar was already sailing the American brig *Clarion* for California. While in Honolulu's harbor, Gyzelaar had overheard the pirates plotting their foul deeds and he was now hurrying to warn his friend, Governor Pablo Vicente de Solá.

And that is where our story begins.

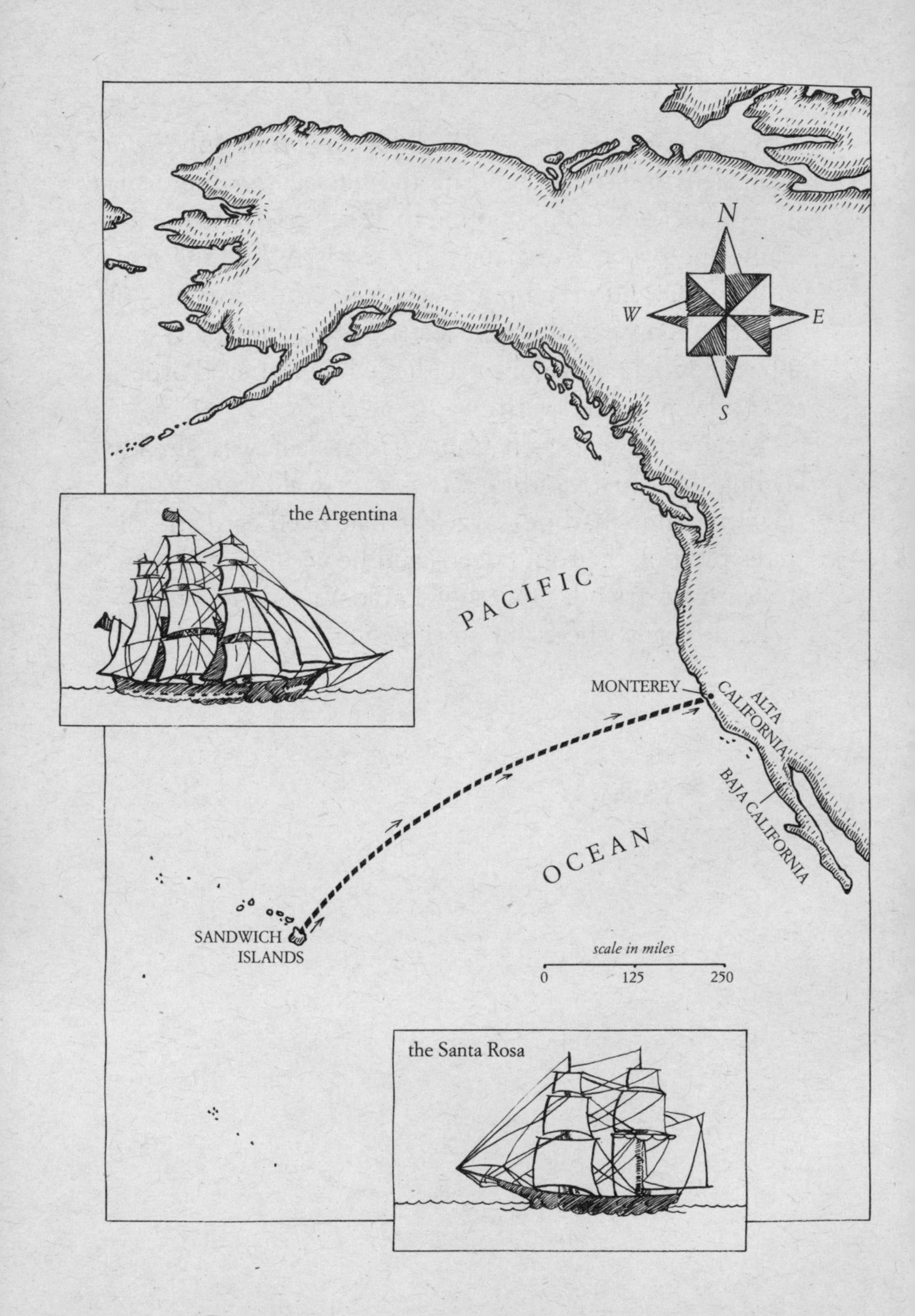
N
W
E
S
the Argentina
PACIFIC
MONTEREY
ALTA
CALIFORNIA
BAJA CALIFORNIA
OCEAN
SANDWICH
ISLANDS
scale in miles
0
125
250
the Santa Rosa

1
The Warning
El aviso

Carlito pulled his hands into the boat when he saw the shark. Its fin sliced the surface of the water as it circled just beyond the kelp bed.

"Papá!"

His father looked up from his nets. He motioned Carlito to sit still, then slowly reached for one of the oars to use as a club.

For many moments they waited. Swells rolled under their *cayuco*, their small fishing boat, lifting it up, then down. From the rocks offshore came the barking of sea lions and the swash of waves. Fog made the air damp, the water gray. When the fin of *el gran tiburón* began moving toward them, Carlito's heart raced and he looked at his father, whose fist tightened on the oar.

Through the murky water they saw the huge white shape, then, inches away from their net, its snout broke the surface. A cold dark eye stared at them as the shark drifted by. Carlito was horrified it had come close enough to touch, and when he realized it was bigger than their *cayuco*, perhaps eighteen feet long, he began to shiver. Suddenly, though, the shark sank from sight, the water rippling above it.

They watched its wake. Carlito knew *el gran tiburón* wanted breakfast, and he knew it was headed for the otters playing in the kelp. A splash and a terrible squeal made Carlito turn away.

"Papá," he said. "Must the shark eat the little otter? Can't it eat something else?"

Papá smiled at his eleven-year-old son. Carlito's brown hair was damp from the fog and he was still shivering. "It is just the way things are, *m'ijo*."

By noon the fog lifted. Monterey Bay sparkled in the October sunlight. So many otters bobbed in the swells, Papá rowed carefully so he wouldn't hurt any with the oars. They had caught sardines, cod, and perch off Punta Piños, where windblown cypresses met the shore, and now they were returning home.

As Carlito watched for sharks, he noticed a small white spot on the horizon. Soon there was no mistaking the sails of *la goleta*, a schooner moving swiftly in the breeze.

"A ship, Papá, look!"

A trumpet sounded from the presidio and with it, drumbeats and shouting soldiers. Children ran barefoot to the beach where Lieutenant José María Estudillo would soon stand with his spyglass and silver megaphone. It was his job to hail the ship's captain and learn his business, for California was owned by Spain. Only friends of King Ferdinand VII would be allowed ashore.

Carlito watched in awe as the three-masted schooner entered the bay. From somewhere on deck a bo's'n's whistle pierced the air. Men high in the rigging quickly furled sails until the masts were bare as twigs. When it seemed *la goleta* would crash onto the beach, another whistle sounded and immediately it veered away, dropping an anchor from its bow.

Fat swells splashed against Papá's oars and into the boat, drenching them. They found themselves pulled directly under the bowsprit of the huge ship. Carlito gazed up at the carved figurehead, a beautiful painted lady with red lips and golden hair. Next to her on the hull, blue lettering spelled the ship's name: *Clarion*.

As Papá rowed away from its towering shadow, they looked up at the mizzenmast where a flag snapped in the breeze. It had red-and-white stripes and a blue square in its upper corner with twenty white stars.

"Yankees," said Papá. "They're probably from Boston like our friend Thomas Doak."

Lieutenant Estudillo waited on the beach surrounded by children who shrieked with excitement, for the arrival of *una goleta* often meant there would be a fiesta. "Ho, schooner," he called in English. "What brings you to our capital city?"

An assortment of officers in uniform gathered on deck as a longboat was lowered over the side. One of the men hailed back, "We come to warn you, señor."

Papá stopped rowing. He shaded his eyes to see the officer better.

Several minutes passed as the first mate asked permission to land and Lieutenant Estudillo consulted his documents. Papá let the *cayuco* drift so he could listen. Three words called out across the water made his jaw tighten. It was the first time Carlito had seen such anger on his father's face.

Again the words were called out: "Pirates are coming."

2
The Young Cowboys

Los jóvenes vaqueros

A small wave pushed the longboat into shore. Four sailors jumped into knee-deep water and dragged it onto the beach. As the *Clarion*'s captain stepped over the bow onto wet sand, an inch of foam washed over his boot. He smiled at Lieutenant Estudillo and extended a hand.

"*Amigo*, friend," Estudillo said when he recognized the captain's blue eyes and yellow beard. Two years earlier Captain Gyzelaar had sailed into Monterey aboard the *Lydia*. Even though he was not Spanish, he liked these Californians and their beautiful village, and had earned their trust.

Captain Gyzelaar was led half a mile up a sandy path to the presidio. Thick adobe walls surrounded a courtyard where two rusty cannons pointed to the gate; above it was the flag of Spain. The church lay directly ahead, the king's warehouses and jail along the left wall, the guardhouse and Governor Solá's office on the right.

Chickens and goats wandered wherever they pleased.

"Amigo," said Governor Solá. He wore the same bicorn hat as the lieutenant, tall black boots, and a waistcoat with fringed epaulets. A sash over his shoulder held his sword in a silver scabbard. The warning of *piratas* had reached him moments earlier.

Cups of warm, thick chocolate were served along with a platter of figs and fried strips of dough called *churros* that had been rolled in cinnamon and sugar. The governor waited patiently while Captain Gyzelaar refreshed himself, for the *Clarion* had been at sea several weeks.

By now the long room was crowded. Children played in the courtyard while their fathers and uncles leaned into windows and doorways. Carlito hurried up the path with Papá. They peered into the room.

Finally the blond captain spoke. "We've come from Honolulu," he began. "My mates and lads were loading sandalwood we bought from King Kamehameha. A black frigate called *Argentina* was anchored near us, as was the *Santa Rosa*, a smaller corvette. I observed their captains in a grog shop enjoying their cups and discussing a wicked plan. Señor, these men are on their way here. They have several hundred soldiers between them, perhaps sixty guns. They are enemies of your king and they plan to destroy what is his."

A murmur rippled through the room to the doorways, then out through the courtyard and among the children who began running through the village. Someone rode horseback a few miles south to Mission San Carlos Borromeo del Rio Carmelo to warn Padre Diego and the other friars.

"Señor?" Carlito called through the crowd. "Are the pirates coming today?"

The captain shook his head. "Not today. Not tomorrow, but soon. The *Argentina* lost much of her crew to scurvy on the voyage from Madagascar, so her captain — his name is Hippolyte de Bouchard — is searching the Sandwich Islands to find natives willing to sail for him. This Bouchard has a bad temper, Señor Solá. I saw him flog a man to death. His hatred for Spain will mean much trouble for you. That is why I came, *amigo*, to warn you."

Captain Gyzelaar took his pipe from his vest pocket. A Costanoan Indian boy brought a tinderbox and with a small pair of tongs set a burning coal on the tobacco. Another boy knelt so the captain could use his back as a footstool.

Papá drew Carlito away from the window. "Come," he said. "We must tell Mamá and Nina. We'll find a safe place for them."

The next few days were frantic as *carretas*, long narrow carts, were loaded with clothing and personal treasures. The schoolmaster, Señor Archuleta, dismissed the children because they were too wild with excitement to do their lessons.

Instead of helping their mothers and aunts, Carlito and his friends ran to their horses grazing outside the village. Amid shouts and whoops they galloped along the beach and through the forests of Punta Piños. They pretended they were fighting pirates, so they took turns lassoing each other with their lariats, then sword fighting with sticks.

At the edge of a cliff they hid in the twisted branches of a cypress to spy on the harbor. When these adventures no longer amused them, the young Spaniards rode through the village to lasso their startled dogs. Geese and chickens scattered out of the sudden dust.

"Pirates are coming," the boys yelled happily to one another. "We are *vaqueros*, they can't hurt us!"

3
A New Dance
Un baile nuevo

Lieutenant Estudillo and Governor Solá stood on a bluff looking out to sea. Each had a brass spyglass.

"Perhaps our friend was mistaken," the lieutenant said. Four weeks had passed with no sign of the pirates. Most of the *carretas* had been unloaded and were being used again to haul wood. The soldiers were so relaxed they played cards and took long *siestas*.

"Or," said the governor, "the ships went down in a storm. That is one possibility. But I'm remembering something our friend said. This Captain Bouchard lost his navigator to scurvy just before Honolulu, so maybe the pirate is lost and can't find his way to Monterey after all."

The men laughed. They were confident the pirates were nowhere near Alta California, because word traveled fast along *El Camino Real*, the Royal Highway. This was the narrow, dusty road connecting the twenty Spanish missions between San Diego and San Francisco, and while there was always a donkey or two ambling along, important news such as this would be brought on galloping horse.

Solá tucked his telescope into his belt. "No," he said, "I can't worry about trouble today. We have a *fandango* to attend. Come."

The dance had already started. Carlito wore a white cotton shirt with red embroidery on the sleeves and collar. A blue satin vest came to his waist, where a red sash held up his trousers. Someday he would be able to wear knee pants with black stockings like Papá.

He watched his mother with the other women, swirling in their bright skirts, then lifting their hands to clap. Stomp, stomp went their feet, which were laced into fine leather shoes barely seen under their ruffled hems. They laughed as their little daughters imitated them nearby.

Mamá was pretty. Her brown hair was swept up into a tall comb with a lace mantle draped down her back. She was light-complected with brown eyes, a pure Castilian. Her beautiful smile caught Carlito. Then she and the others began to sing; it was a new song called "*La Remadora*, the Oarswoman," and it went like this:

"*¡Vienen los insurgentes, pero no sabemos cuándo!* The rebels are coming but we don't know when!" Stomp-stomp, clap-clap. 'Round and 'round. Stomp-stomp. Clap-clap. How colorful dancing women look, thought

Carlito, how graceful. They were like *las mariposas*, the butterflies that cover the trees during winter near Punta Piños. Some of the littlest girls, including Carlito's sister, Nina, danced in elegant skirts of black and orange because they wanted to imitate the flying wings.

The dance became more lively as men joined in with castanets and tambourines. Carlito loved the way his parents looked at each other as they turned and stepped, then turned. Music from guitars and *las gaitas*, the Spanish bagpipes, could be heard for miles. Costanoans working the fields near the mission stopped to listen, but only for a moment because they knew they might be flogged.

Late afternoon Carlito's family returned home. Their whitewashed adobe looked pink from the sunset and the red-tiled roof held warmth from the day. Iron grates covered the windows, but no glass. The two small rooms with dirt floors were simply furnished: three beds, a few chairs, one table, a looking glass on one side of the door, a crucifix on the other. There was no fireplace, only candlelight to warm them. A small kitchen was twenty feet away from the adobe, a protection against fire.

This evening Carlito's newly wed uncle and aunt, tío Roberto and tía Juanita, ate with them. There was a round loaf of bread, goat's milk cheese, beans, and *gazpacho*: a cool soup made from tomatoes, cucumbers, olive oil, and garlic. It was a delicious meal and by the time his mother and aunt lit their cigars, Carlito felt sleepy. He heard their laughter as tío Roberto told a story, but the next thing Carlito knew, the room was quiet and dark, and he was under his blanket. Strips of moonlight slanted in through a window across his bed.

He listened. There was the familiar sound of his sleeping family: rhythmic breathing and his father's light snore; in the distance there was the usual noise of sea lions. Something had awakened him, but what?

Carlito slid his feet into his *zapatos* and pushed back the hide that covered their door. A cold breeze met him. His breath made frost as he hurried between adobes to where he could see the bay. Waves rolled so gently onto the beach it seemed the ocean was a great silvery pond.

When Carlito looked south toward Punta Piños, he froze. For there in the moonlight, anchored quietly, were two ships. There was no mistaking one of them: *la fragata negra*, the black frigate.

The cannon ports on both hulls were open and even from the distance Carlito could see movement on deck.

4
The Black Frigate

La fragata negra

Carlito knew he must stay calm. He hurried up the road, slipped through the doorway, and knelt by his sleeping father. Gently he touched his shoulder.

Papá bolted awake. When Carlito pressed his finger to his lips, Papá got out of bed without a word. He followed Carlito outside, down the road, until they stopped in the shadow of a *carreta.*

When Papá saw the ships, he shook his head sadly. *"¡Jesucristo!"* he whispered, crossing himself. He turned to his son and gripped his shoulders. There were tears in Papá's eyes. *"M'ijo,"* he said. "Go wake your uncle, I'll get Señor Solá. We must be absolutely quiet, do you understand?"

"Yes, Papá."

"As long as the pirates think we're sleeping we have some time to protect ourselves. Now hurry."

Carlito's feet made no sound in the soft dirt. Soon tío

Roberto was on his way with many others.

Candlelight glowed from Solá's window. The presidio commander, Sergeant Manuel Gómez, was furious he hadn't been first to spot the pirates. He threw up his hands. "What do you mean, the cannons aren't ready?" he yelled to his corporal, José Vallejo.

Solá stepped between the men and said, "There's no time to blame. We must work together. Now, this is what we'll do."

Within an hour the entire village knew about the ships.

In the early morning darkness the *carretas* once again were loaded. Sleeping babies were tucked into baskets and older children helped with younger ones. Husbands embraced tearful wives. Mamá begged Papá to come with her.

"Please don't go to the fort, Timoteo," she said. "You are only a poor fisherman who knows nothing of war. Please."

"I must help the others, darling. You'll be safe at Bautista Mission and besides, Carlito will be with you. I'll follow as soon as possible."

Carlito watched his parents hold each other as Nina hid herself in Mamá's wide skirt. He wanted to be the man of the family and drive the *carreta* to safety, but he also wanted to watch the ships.

As Carlito helped adjust the heavy wooden yoke for their oxen, he reasoned to himself. Papá hadn't actually ordered him to stay with Mamá, so maybe it was all right if he didn't.

By sunrise the road into the woods leading east to Mission San Juan Bautista was crowded and traffic moved slowly. Women called to each other and there was much confusion as children ran nervously from family to family.

Carlito found his cousin. "I have man business to take care of," he told the younger boy, making him promise to look after Nina. When Carlito started to explain all this to Mamá, she smiled at him so tenderly he forgot his words. How could he tell her he was leaving?

Minutes later, while she was passing out *churros* to the younger children, he ran from the forest to the beach. Along the path he caught up to one of his friends, Ziba, who also had run away from his mother.

The two of them arrived as a fifteen-foot sailboat surfed into shore. Six of the roughest men Carlito had ever seen sloshed through the waves to pull the cutter out. They wore rings in their ears, had tattoos, and their hair was pulled back into pigtails that were stiff and black with tar. One man was bald. Hanging from his belt was a dagger that glinted in the sunlight. Carlito was fascinated to see a boy with them. A patch covered his left eye and there was a pink scar running from his left ear to his chin. What was a boy his age doing on a pirate ship? Carlito wondered.

An officer in blue uniform stepped out of the boat, carrying a white flag. Tucked under his arm was a rolled parchment with a red string tied around it. The crowd of Californians parted as the flag of truce moved toward the presidio.

Governor Solá did not smile, nor offer the man a seat. He waited.

"Sir, I am Peter Corney," the man said in English, "first in command aboard the *Santa Rosa*. Captain Bouchard of the *Argentina* has a message for you."

Carlito and Ziba slipped unnoticed into the governor's quarters. They could see Papá, tío Roberto, and four of Carlito's other uncles speaking to Corporal Vallejo. The men fell silent when Captain Corney began unrolling the letter.

"Begging your pardon, sir, but as I'm a born-and-bred Englishman, I do not understand Spanish. Here."

Solá's eyes narrowed. He took the letter and held it in front of him, reading aloud in Spanish:

> "To the commandant of the port of Monterey. Dear Sir:
>
> "Since the king of Spain has declared bloody war on my country Argentina, I am making a defense by waging war on land and sea and every port King Ferdinand dares to call his own.
>
> "Therefore, having crossed the Pacific Ocean to this coast, I now desire the surrender of your city with all the furniture and other belongings of the king. If you do not do so,

the city will be reduced to cinders, and also the other surrounding villages. It is within my power to bring about this destruction.

"You may evade all the above spilling of blood by agreeing to my proposal. If so, I shall desist from what I say. Be good enough to reply to me as soon as possible.

"May God keep you many years.

"Signed, Hippolyte de Bouchard, aboard the *Argentina*. Dated November 23, 1818."

When Governor Solá finished reading, he rolled up the letter and handed it to Sergeant Gómez. With his right hand he gave Captain Corney a brisk salute. In English he said, "We will respond by sunrise tomorrow."

Then the dignified governor folded his hands in front of him, and in a soft voice he said to Captain Corney, in Spanish, "You are garbage. Get your filthy face out of my sight."

5

An Angry Response

Una respuesta enojada

All eyes were on the English captain as he returned to the beach where his sailors and the one-eyed boy stood guard. They raised the cutter's mainsail and jib and soon were sailing to the outer bay where the black frigate waited.

Solá turned to his officers and the villagers. "I'll dictate a response, but I need someone with perfect handwriting to help me." The governor did not want anyone to see that his hands were shaking.

The room was quiet. With the exception of the mission padres and some of the friars, most adult Montereyans were illiterate, and those who could read and write had not perfected their penmanship.

"Señor?" The small voice was Carlito's. Papá turned around. He stared at his son with a mixture of surprise and anger. *What are you doing here?* his eyes said.

"*Gracias*, Carlito," Solá said, motioning the boy to come sit at his desk. "Señor Archuleta has told me you are one of his best pupils. Here." He dipped a quill into a small jug of ink and handed it to Carlito with a square of fresh parchment.

When they finished, Carlito had to read what had been dictated. He glanced at his father and was relieved to see a look that said, *Go ahead, we'll talk later.*

Carlito read:

> "To the commander of the frigate *Argentina*. Dear Sir: The governor looks with due scorn upon all that Bouchard's communication contained.
>
> "The great monarch whom I serve had confided to me his command to defend Monterey and keep it under his rule. If you should use force as threatened, I with mine will make you know the honor and firmness with which I will repel you.
>
> "And while there is a man alive in the province you will not succeed in your plan of taking possession since all its inhabitants are faithful servants of the king, and will shed the last drop of blood in his service."

Carlito looked up. When the governor nodded his approval the quiet men burst into cheers. "*¡Viva el rey!* Long live the king!"

As Sergeant Gómez assembled his men, Papá led Carlito across the courtyard to the church. It was cold inside, even though many clusters of candles cast a warm glow. They crossed themselves as they knelt down in a pew.

For several moments Papá's eyes were closed, his head bowed. Finally he looked at his son.

"You disobeyed me, *m'ijo.*"

"But Papá, you didn't say . . ."

". . . Carlito. My wishes were that you help your mother and sister. That alone should have been enough. But now it's too dangerous to travel so you must stay with me. Can you understand, *m'ijo*, that Mamá must be sick with worry, that she has neither husband nor son to comfort her?"

There was silence between them. Carlito felt miserable. How could he have been so selfish?

Papá put his arm around his son and nodded toward the altar where a carving of Jesus looked down at them. He began to pray. "The Lord is my shepherd . . ."

The night passed slowly. Nearly eighty soldiers and villagers worked together through the long hours before dawn, careful not to give themselves away by candlelight. Extra gunpowder was carried to the fort where ten twelve-pound cannons pointed through the wall facing the sea. Three more were rolled down to the beach near Punta Piños. Here Ensign José Estrada waited through the cold, damp night with a small group of fishermen who knew nothing of guns, but only that they were servants of the king. They would not let pirates capture their beautiful Monterey.

In the presidio courtyard three Costanoan girls tended

a small cooking fire where men came to warm themselves with strong black coffee and corn cakes. After Governor Solá made sure Carlito and Ziba had eaten, he invited them to help him. They climbed to the top of the bell tower where they could watch the dark sea. The moon was hidden by clouds, and a cold wind blew up their sleeves as they looked through spyglasses.

A small glow on the *Santa Rosa* showed where a lantern hung, swaying with the swells that rocked the ships. Across the black stern of the *Argentina* were yellow squares of light from Hippolyte de Bouchard's quarters.

"The pirate captain is not sleeping," said Carlito to the governor.

"Yes, *m'ijo*, you are correct."

Before sunrise the cutter came ashore. This time Corney's first lieutenant, Mr. Woodburn, marched up the path. As soon as Sergeant Gómez handed him the governor's letter, Mr. Woodburn saluted, then returned to the beach. The sky began to turn grayish-pink as the little boat cut through the waves back toward the frigate.

Governor Solá watched through his glass as Lieutenant Woodburn climbed up the ship's rope ladder, walked to the quarterdeck, then disappeared down the companionway where Bouchard waited.

Moments later the governor saw a puff of smoke from one of the gun ports, followed by a thud, then a tremendous splash offshore. Another thud and part of the presidio wall exploded in a shower of bricks.

6
"Murderer!"

"¡Asesino!"

Ziba and Carlito had fallen asleep in the tower, curled into a corner on the floor, protected from the wind. The explosion brought them to their feet in a panic. They could see the two ships sailing closer to the beach with cannons firing.

"What should we do?" cried Ziba. "Where is Señor Solá, where did our fathers go?"

"I don't know, I don't know," Carlito said.

As the boys looked out over the bay their horror increased. While cannons continued to blast, the *Santa Rosa* lowered five boats filled with pirates and Sandwich Islanders wearing only loincloths. In moments they splashed ashore and ran up the beach shouting and waving knives. The islanders carried spears.

"They're coming, get down," said Carlito, pulling his friend to the floor. They peered through a small rain-spout. The Spaniards returned fire. Cannons from both sides filled the air with smoke; the noise was deafening.

Directly below the boys came the sounds of wood splintering and pottery being thrown against walls. Loud voices cursed.

Carlito grabbed Ziba's arm and motioned him to be silent. They pressed themselves into the corner and dared not look down the ladder. They knew without seeing that men were in the church and they were destroying it.

Someone screamed that the *Santa Rosa* had been hit, which drew the buccaneers out of the church and down to the beach. Carlito peeked over the tower ledge to see flames on the ship's deck, a mast snapped in two, and spars torn through rigging. There was a gaping hole just above the waterline.

"Bravo!" cried Ziba. As two cutters began rowing back to the ship, Carlito stood up and also cried, "Bravo!"

But his cheer immediately turned to panic. Six boats from the black frigate were almost to Punta Piños. Dozens of marines and more Sandwich Islanders were about to land. Was Ensign Estrada still there with his cannons? Carlito wondered. Did the fishermen know what to do?

Carlito's throat tightened. Papá. Could it be that Papá had gone with Estrada?

"We must hurry," he said as he urged Ziba down the wobbly ladder, spyglasses tucked into their waistbands. "Our fathers need us."

Carlito knew in his heart that two boys could not fight so many pirates, but still they ran until they reached the cliff. They climbed into the branches of their secret tree to watch the rocky beach below. The cannons were there, but Señor Estrada and the fishermen were retreating into the woods, trying to outrun those who had jumped from the boats into shallow water.

An officer wearing a bicorn hat and dress coat raised a musket and fired. One of the fishermen threw his arms in the air, then fell to the sand. Another shot hit a man in the shoulder, but he kept running.

Carlito wrapped himself around a branch so he could look through his glass without falling. His eye caught the blue collar of the officer's coat and his long red hair, which was tied back with string. The coat disappeared behind a bluff so Carlito turned to the beach.

A small wave washed over the man's legs, then out again. He lay on his side in the wet sand, blood staining the water's edge. When Carlito focused on the man's face, the open eyes that no longer held life, he gave an anguished cry.

"No, please, no! Papá . . . Papá . . ."

7
Revenge
Venganza

The roar of waves drowned out Carlito's cries as he clung to the branch. For many minutes he wept and shook his head with disbelief.

"Why, why?" he sobbed.

Ziba rubbed his friend's arm, trying to comfort him while coaxing him out of the tree. "Carlito, we can't stay here. They'll find us. Come."

They hid in the woods. In the distance came the thuds of cannon fire and an occasional explosion. Carlito had stopped crying, but his heart was so heavy he could not speak. They were near the grove of butterflies. Wings of black and orange fluttered into view as the boys ran.

Ahead was a stray horse dragging its reins. Ziba helped Carlito into the saddle, then leaped up behind and took the road to Mission San Juan Bautista. Carlito felt sick in his soul because he suddenly realized that he must tell Mamá.

When he saw her standing by their *carreta*, his eyes filled. She was overjoyed to see him.

"M'ijo, m'ijo," she cried, lifting the edge of her skirt to run to him. But as she saw his sorrow, heard his broken words, she covered her face with her hands. Friends instantly surrounded her, some pleading with Carlito for details, but he could say no more. Tío Roberto, who had stayed with the family when Carlito turned up missing, pulled the stricken boy into his arms.

There was much weeping that day, for word came that two more husbands had been killed, fathers of Carlito's friends. Late afternoon the families gathered in the mission chapel to be consoled by Padre Rodriguez, but they were interrupted by the rumble of galloping hooves.

Spanish soldiers escorted Governor Solá, who brought terrible news. "All is lost," the governor cried. "*Piratas* have captured Monterey . . . our beautiful Monterey . . ." From his saddlebag he brought out the only thing he was able to save: the archives. When he held the rolled parchments to his chest, the gentle governor lowered his head and sobbed.

Carlito and Ziba walked along the broad stream that flowed beyond the mission. Several younger boys followed them, splashing through the water and hoping to hear more about the murder and about the pirates.

"I'm going to avenge my father's death," Carlito said without looking at the faces turned toward him. He held a smooth stone in his hand, remembering stories the padres told. "David slew Goliath. I will slay the red-haired man."

In the middle of the night Ziba, Carlito, and four others slipped into the woods, untethered their horses, and rode bareback to the edge of Monterey. They hid among the dark trees.

Torches planted in the sand made the village glow. There was drunken laughter as the thieves ransacked each home and shop, then stumbled to the beach, arms full. One by one the ships' boats sailed out to the *Argentina* and *Santa Rosa*, loaded with small personal treasures the Montereyans had been unable to rescue. Damage to the *Santa Rosa* was above the waterline so it hadn't sunk.

The Sandwich Islanders were no longer half naked, for they had found chests of fine Spanish clothing. The boys were enraged to see these huge men wearing their mothers' dresses and shawls, their lace mantles. Dainty satin shoes had been tied together to make necklaces, and men's pantaloons were wrapped around their wide waists. Several wore children's *sombreros*, which resembled tiny cups on their heads. To Carlito, such a giant was not as frightening as before.

On the ships, lantern light cast shadows of men carrying aboard their booty. They fired guns in the air, hoping to keep away the villagers. Every few minutes a cannon boomed, followed by a deep splash.

The boys dozed in the trees. At dawn they were awakened by Scottish bagpipes, a drum, and a fife. To their amazement, a victory band marched along the cold beach, led by two bare-chested pirates carrying flags. One flag was red, meaning "no quarter," that Spaniards were forbidden in Monterey; the other was black with a white skull.

As the musicians paraded into town Carlito made his plan.

8
A Terrible Mistake
Una equivocación terrible

Just after midnight, on the fourth night Monterey was occupied by buccaneers, Carlito led his friends, five in all, to their secret cove. Here was Papá's *cayuco*, and one other small craft. They knew what to do so no one spoke. Each boy carried a knife and wore his lariat like a shoulder sash. A copper tinderbox filled with hot coals was put into each boat.

When tío Roberto had asked where they were going, Carlito lied. If the uncles and fathers knew they were not really rounding up a bullock for meat, they would have never let the boys leave the mission.

They rowed through the dark swells. A cold mist hid the two little boats from sight as they neared the ships. Carlito's *cayuco* bumped against the thick wet rope that stretched down from the frigate's bow. He grabbed it as Ziba pulled in the oars. On a deck high above them was laughter and the thumps of men dancing to a fife.

Carlito's heart sank. He'd counted on the pirates being asleep in their beds. And he'd made another mistake, a terrible mistake, but he didn't dare tell his friends.

This had been his plan: Since each ship had one anchor off the bow, the young Spaniards would cut the lines and set fire to the ragged ends. The tide would carry the burning vessels to sea where all would perish, including the red-haired officer. And if any escaped, the boys would capture them with their lariats.

What Carlito hadn't remembered was how huge the anchor ropes were: twenty-two inches around, nearly the thickness of his own body. To cut one would take hours.

Also, in Carlito's grief and his hurry to want his enemy dead, he'd forgotten an important detail: Ships' ropes at the waterline are soaking wet. A torch would not start them burning and certainly coals from a tinderbox would not.

He was furious with himself and even more angry with his friends. Why hadn't they helped him think things through? Just because his father was murdered he had suddenly become a hero, a leader no one questioned. What would his friends think about their leader now? he wondered.

Carlito knelt in the boat, his arm still hooked around the dripping rope that rose and sank in the swells. He whispered a new plan and prayed the other boys would think to do the same. While Ziba and Pedro held fast, Carlito shinned up to where the line was not as wet, about five feet above the water's surface, and with his knife began sawing at the twisted hemp. If they couldn't set the ships on fire they could at least set them adrift, even if it took them all night.

After ten minutes, though, Carlito's arms and legs ached and he was shivering from cold. A wind had come up. Waves splashed him each time the frigate's bow dipped toward the rising sea. Exhausted, he lay his head against the scratchy rope, but a sudden cry made him look down. To his horror Pedro had fallen overboard.

Ziba had let go of the anchor line and was frantically reaching into the water to pull Pedro back in. For a moment Carlito considered throwing them his lariat but he, too, might lose his balance and fall. He watched helplessly as the swift current took them. In seconds a cresting wave carried the little boat into the fog.

9
Billy Bumpus
Billy Bumpus

Carlito closed his eyes.

He could jump in and swim the half mile to shore, but the water was cold and so rough he feared he would drown. Also, he knew that below him, swimming silently in the dark water was *el gran tiburón*, who would enjoy eating a boy as much as he would an otter.

And even if Ziba rescued Pedro, could they row against such a strong current, back to where Carlito clung?

The wind rocked him as if he were on horseback. Carlito wanted to be brave, but he struggled to keep from crying. *Papá dead . . . his poor mother . . . where were his friends?* He forced himself to push aside these thoughts, as if closing a door to a noisy room. He must move forward before he became too stiff to move at all.

He inched upward. The rope prickled through his wet shirt. Twelve feet above the waterline was an opening into the ship for the anchor line, the hawsehole, just big enough for him to crawl through.

When his hands touched wood he boosted himself inside, tumbling down to a damp floor. He tried to stand, but the ceiling was so low he hit his head. A lantern swinging from a beam cast shadows between rows of cannons, thirty-two-pounders pointing out the gun ports toward Monterey.

Directly in front of him was a large pen with three hogs and four sheep. Voices made Carlito crouch low and when a man's shadow stretched toward him he crawled into the hay. It was soggy and smelled bad. He was so exhausted, though, he managed to fall asleep.

Several hours later he woke to something pulling his hair. Too afraid to move, he opened his eyes. A large, gray rat nestled by Carlito's shoulder, another nibbled at his sleeve. As two others ran over his legs, he bolted upright and found himself face-to-face with a boy holding a club. It was the one-eyed boy he'd seen on the beach.

They stared at each other. The boy's scar was shiny in the lamplight and there were two gold hoops in his left ear. Next to him was a man holding a lantern over the pen. He was bald with a long black beard that had been split into two braids.

"You a Spaniard?" the man asked in English. His name was Simeon.

Carlito nodded. He had learned some English from Yankee sailors who'd jumped ship in Monterey. Governor Solá allowed them to remain if they were baptized Catholics and became Spanish citizens. One of Carlito's friends was Thomas Doak, a carpenter from Boston who had married the beautiful María Lugarda.

"My name is Carlito José Domínguez and I am a servant of the king." These were words he had practiced with Thomas, words that now made the man and the boy laugh.

"Ha," said Simeon. "You may well be Carlito so-and-so, but right now you are a stowaway aboard the *Argentina*. Captain Bouchard hates your king and he thinks even less of stowaways. The last one he found had his lips sewn shut, then he was dangled over the side until the sharks found him, so what d'ye think about that, laddie?"

Carlito didn't answer. He had already removed his knife from his waist and was now hiding it in the straw with his lariat.

The boy motioned Carlito to get up, then said, "And the stowaway before him had an eye put out and his throat slit, but he lived to tell about it. He lived to become the ship's official rat killer. That boy's name is Billy Bumpus and you're looking at 'im."

10
The Captain
El capitán

Carlito climbed out of the pen. His cotton pants were soaked with dung and his hair was sticky. He stumbled toward the hawsehole, then leaned out to gulp fresh air. It was nearly daybreak. Fog made the rolling sea look gray.

He felt a growing terror as he realized he was now a captive. Why hadn't he tried to swim for shore? Far better to drown than be tortured by pirates.

"Laddie, there's only one way to save your neck. Follow us."

Carrying the lantern, Simeon led them alongside the anchor rope, which lay stretched out like a giant python. He passed a row of cannons, stooping to avoid bumping his head. In the shadows were men, quiet as cockroaches. Some slept in hammocks strung between beams, others watched Carlito with suspicion. The blade of a sword shone briefly, then disappeared.

When they reached the companionway, Billy Bumpus

turned to Carlito. He leaned close, pushing the club into his neck. "Do as we say or we'll beat you like a rat and no one'll know the difference."

Carlito kept his eyes down. "All right," he whispered in English. He didn't understand why this boy was mean, but he did believe his threat. He moved forward. Only when Simeon began to climb the narrow steps did Carlito notice the man's wooden leg. It was decorated with ornate carvings like scrimshaw.

Under the low ceiling of the middle deck were more cannons, twenty-four-pounders. A foul smell introduced Carlito to the sick bay, where putrid vinegar was being used as a disinfectant. On a table, held down by four mates, was a screaming soldier about to have both hands amputated. The floor was sticky with blood.

Simeon pointed to the surgeon, an obese man in stained clothing. "Your Spanish guns did this. The captain buried five yesterday and now he's even more furious than when he read your governor's ridiculous letter."

They continued along the middle deck aft, toward the stern, past the galley where all food was prepared. Just beyond was the mainmast rising up from the hold like a huge tree. Everywhere Carlito looked were crates and barrels, ropes and tools, thick folds of canvas for the sailmaker. Soldiers cleaning muskets stared at him. There were more hammocks with sleeping men, another pen with two lambs and one milk cow. A goat roaming by helped himself to someone's biscuit, then hurriedly mounted the stairs.

Overhead were thuds from men working on deck, creaks and groans from the hull itself. A murmur of voices seemed to be in every corner, which made Carlito realize there were hundreds of men aboard. The *Santa Rosa* must have nearly as many, also. No wonder the pirates were able to capture Monterey.

Simeon led them through a maze of barrels, ducking his head here, stepping over coils of rope there. Up eight steps, around the base of the mizzenmast, down four steps then along a narrow corridor. He stopped in front of a mahogany door and rapped three times.

"Who calls?" came an angry voice.

"Simeon and Bumpus, sir, requesting permission to speak to the captain. Sir."

Carlito felt himself begin to sweat. His stomach tightened. Was this *el capitán pirata*, the pirate captain? He was too nervous to ask. For one long minute they waited.

Finally the voice said, "Enter."

They ducked under the low doorway. Before them stood a man in a commodore's uniform. He was leaning over a table on which charts were spread out. He did not look up. The breakfast tray next to him was untouched. Carlito was so hungry the sight of coffee and a meat sandwich made the back of his mouth water.

He glanced around the room. At the stern a wall of windows opened to a wide view of the bay and the wooded hills of Monterey. He could see the beach where two cutters were being launched into the waves. Their cargo: sheep, hogs, and chickens. Barrels of fresh water were being towed to the ships.

"You are wasting my time," said the man, studying Carlito's clothes, "and my quarters are beginning to stink. What is a Spaniard doing aboard my vessel?"

Billy spoke. "Captain Bouchard, sir. This is your new cabin boy like you asked for, to replace the boy lost at sea. Sir."

"Ha." Bouchard held out his hands to admire his new rings of ruby and gold, then he slammed a fist on the table. The cup bounced, spilling coffee onto the floor. "Already you have failed, Spaniard."

Carlito was speechless. He raised his shoulders with question.

"You have failed because there is a mess by my feet and you are standing there like a stupid pig farmer."

Sweat gathered on Simeon's bald head. Through clenched teeth he said, "Use that rag of a shirt you're wearing. Now."

Carlito peeled his shirt over his head then knelt on the wood floor. The roll of the ship made the puddle spread. He mopped it up, and quickly backed away from the boots he feared might kick him. His face burned with shame, with a growing rage.

Bouchard faced them. He had dark eyes and oily black hair. His chin was plump. Staring at Carlito, his mouth moved into a tight smile.

"I am master of this ship," he said. "You will do as I command. If you show any loyalty to your king you will be flogged, then dragged beneath the keel until the sharks finish you off. Remember one thing, Spaniard: No one can serve two masters."

In that instant Carlito decided he would never again clean the floor for this man. As soon as darkness fell he would swim to shore, even if it meant getting caught by *el gran tiburón*.

11
A City Burns

Arde una ciudad

Carlito stood at attention while Simeon and Billy Bumpus pointed around the captain's cabin explaining his duties. His wet shirt stuck to his back. He was cold and hungry.

And he was sad. *Las gaviotas*, the seagulls, hovering outside the windows made him think of his father. Their sharp cries reminded him of when he and Papá pulled in their nets and their *cayuco* would be surrounded by noisy, diving birds. But these were pirate gulls, eating garbage dumped from a gun port two decks below.

While Bouchard watched, Carlito bent to his first chore. Beside the swinging bed was a cabinet with a washbasin. Underneath was a chamber pot, full. He gagged at the smell. Carefully Carlito carried it out the door, into the hallway, then around the corner to the wardroom quarter gallery, which resembled an outhouse extended over the waves. Carefully he poured, the contents splashing into the water below. This was to be done before breakfast each morning, followed by a scrubbing of the seat and floor.

Carlito was also to serve Bouchard's quartermaster, whose cabin was down the steps. Anything the two men ordered, he was to obey. Simeon knocked on the door and identified himself. A sour voice answered.

They entered a small room at the stern with two windows above the bed. This officer was fastening the silver buttons of his coat, which was cut to the waist in front, to the knees in back. When he turned toward them, Carlito gasped.

There stood the man who had killed his father.

His red hair was swept back from his forehead and hung below his shoulders. His eyes were icy blue. He put his hand on the hilt of his sword and glared at Carlito. "Does the captain know you've brought vermin aboard his vessel?" he asked Simeon.

"Aye, Mr. Parvo. But this Spaniard's with us; he begged the captain t'take him aboard, he did." Simeon casually stroked the two braids of his beard as if lying was his everyday business.

Carlito felt color rise to his cheeks. How he hated this red-haired man. He wanted to grab the sword and run it through Parvo's heart.

A high-pitched whistle interrupted them. Parvo hurriedly put on his hat and shouldered his way between them. As he ducked through the narrow doorway he turned briefly to address Carlito. His upper teeth were black at the gums and his breath stank of onion.

"The last boy your size had an unfortunate tumble out that window there. Poor lad."

A sudden lurch of the ship made Carlito lose his balance. He clutched the doorjamb as Parvo disappeared around a dark corner, with Simeon and Billy Bumpus close behind.

"All hands on deck," Billy called, "and that means you, too, Spaniard."

Carlito felt desperate as he realized the black frigate was preparing to sail. He came to the capstan, the huge wheel lying on its side with twelve long spokes. Sailors strained to push these spokes, moving clockwise to wind up the cable connected to the massive anchor line.

Carlito stumbled down the companionway back to the sheep pen where he'd hidden his knife and lariat. Here the rope moved along the floor like a wet snake, inching its way out of the water. He wanted to crawl out the hawsehole, but feared he would be crushed.

In a panic he ran to one of the gun ports and tried to squeeze his shoulders beside the cannon so he could dive overboard. There was fresh air on his face, but when he saw the beach he stopped himself. Flames raced along driftwood at the high-water mark and up through the narrow streets. Houses were on fire. Smoke billowed out of the church tower.

Carlito lay his head on the cold steel of the cannon. He felt defeated. His home, his Monterey, was in ruins. He was trapped on a pirate ship and, worst of all, he would never see his family again.

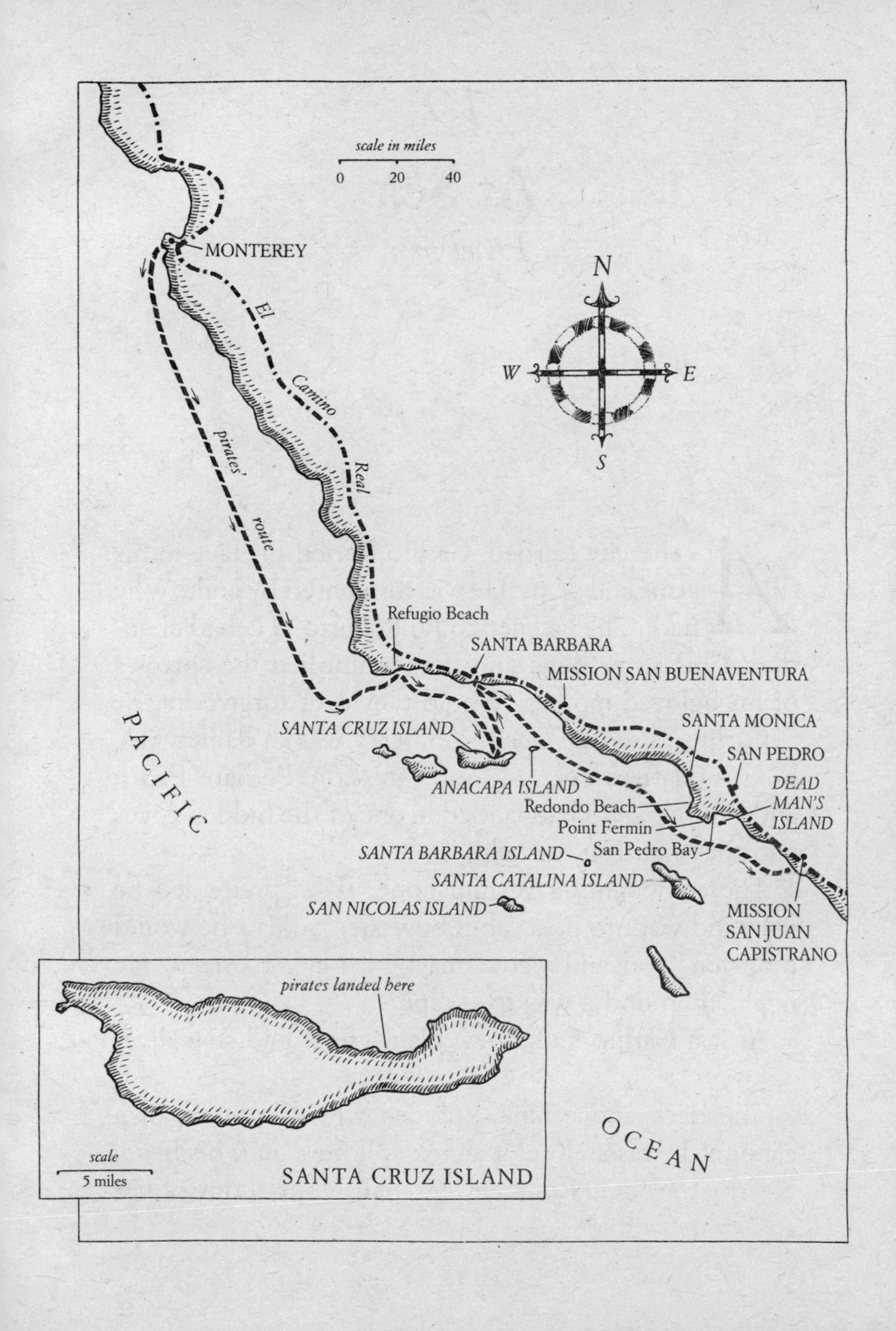
scale in miles
0
20
40
MONTEREY
N
W
E
S
El
Camino
Real
pirates'
route
Refugio Beach
SANTA BARBARA
MISSION SAN BUENAVENTURA
SANTA MONICA
SAN PEDRO
DEAD MAN'S ISLAND
SANTA CRUZ ISLAND
ANACAPA ISLAND
Redondo Beach
Point Fermin
San Pedro Bay
SANTA BARBARA ISLAND
SANTA CATALINA ISLAND
SAN NICOLAS ISLAND
MISSION SAN JUAN CAPISTRANO
PACIFIC
OCEAN
pirates landed here
scale
5 miles
SANTA CRUZ ISLAND

12
At Sea
En el mar

As the city burned, Carlito buried his face in his arms and wept. He was tormented by guilt. Why hadn't he listened to tío Roberto? He had abandoned his sister Nina and now multiplied the sorrows of his beloved mother. Would they ever forgive him?

Carlito raised his head. Monterey was in flames, yes, but his relatives were safe at the mission. Perhaps Pedro and Ziba's *cayuco* had landed in one of the hidden coves and they had run for help.

These thoughts gave him hope. If he pretended he truly did want to be a cabin boy, then at least he would be given food and water, maybe a place to sleep. He might then find a way to escape.

At last Carlito had a new plan: He would stay alive.

The deck above him exploded with the boom of a cannon. It was so loud it shook splinters onto his head. Nearby the *Santa Rosa*, newly repaired, fired one of her guns. Cheers and cries of *"huzza!"* rose from the men aboard both ships. They had finished their dirty business with Monterey and were setting out to sea.

It was December 1, 1818.

Carlito was used to boats so the motion of the sea didn't make him sick. Finally he found his way to the main deck and stood in the cold, salty breeze, rubbing his arms for warmth. The sun was still low in the morning sky.

He looked around in amazement. The ship was as crowded and busy as a village on market day. Men worked at ropes and pulleys, singing in a language he'd never heard; others were on their knees scrubbing the deck with blocks of stone. They were dressed like those he'd seen on shore, in white trousers, shirts open at the neck, and a variety of brightly colored sashes. They had tattoos. Some wore ear hoops. Those who weren't bald had coated their hair with tar to keep it from blowing in their faces. At least two men wore an eye patch like Billy Bumpus's.

There was an assortment of faces from all parts of the world, and different languages being hollered about. Carlito wondered how any of them could understand what to do. To his surprise three Sandwich Islanders hoisting a crate smiled at him. Their stolen shirts looked small on their large bodies.

Carlito gazed up. High above deck, sailors perched along the spars of the three masts. They held on with one hand while loosening lines with the other, their feet balanced on a thin rope. At the signal of the bo's'n's whistle, the tightly rolled canvases fell like sheets and the helmsman turned the wheel to catch the wind.

With a series of loud thumps, fourteen sails filled and bellied out like beautiful white clouds. When Carlito felt the ship speed forward he laughed with exhilaration, momentarily forgetting his troubles.

The *Argentina* and *Santa Rosa* plowed through the waves with the grace and rhythm of horses cantering along the beach. Spray misted the air. Soon they rounded Punta Piños and nothing more could be seen of Monterey except small columns of smoke rising into the blue sky. They sailed south, the forested shoreline on the left, the great rolling Pacific on the right.

Carlito didn't want to be caught idle. He imitated an older boy by trying to twist rope around one of the belaying pins that passed through holes in the rail by the mainmast. While doing this he saw Billy Bumpus. He was dipping a cup into a water barrel, then he offered a drink to Parvo. They seemed to be talking about him.

Billy came alongside and took Carlito's rope. By turning his wrist he showed how to correctly coil it onto the long wooden pin; uncoiled, it would release a line to the mainsail. He tilted his face to look at Carlito with his good eye, then pointed up to the highest yardarm.

"If you're sloppy again, Spaniard, Parvo will make you spend the night up there lashed to the rigging. Hurry, he wants me to show you the head."

He followed Billy to the bow of the ship, then down two steps to a small, A-shaped platform that extended over the waves. Benches with holes for sitting on were along the railing, and three seats were already occupied. Wind blew the odors forward.

"Six lashes," said Billy, "for any man or boy who's found relieving himself other than here. Two dozen for using an officer's privy.

"We live like kings here, compared to them," he continued, now pointing across the swells to the smaller ship. Carlito could see the *Santa Rosa*'s head was merely a rope stretched under the bowsprit. One sailor sat there bare-bottomed, clinging to another rope as waves splashed his feet. When finished, he reached for the line dangling in the water; its soggy end was shared by all the mates to clean themselves.

Carlito looked at Billy. His face was young and freckled, his tangled hair the color of hay. *He's my age*, Carlito thought, and suddenly instead of feeling afraid, he felt bold. He would try to make friends with him.

In careful English he said, "Can I look under your patch, Billy?"

13
The Prisoner
El prisionero

The eye socket was empty and red. The knife that had cut Billy's face and throat had also taken out the eye.

"Who did this to you?" Carlito demanded. "He deserves to die."

Billy smiled sadly. "He did die. Come with me, Spaniard."

The brig was on the lowest deck, below the waterline. Billy's lantern pushed aside the shadows as the boys weaved their way among the dark corridors. Rats scurried out of their path, their claws clicking along the floor and rafters.

Billy stopped. He held the lantern high. There in front of them was a large iron cage with a man standing eagerly at the bars. His beard was nearly to his waist and there were sores on his bare arms. A bad smell came from the straw.

"God bless you, Billy," the man said.

Carlito was shocked to see such a starved person and even more shocked when the man and Billy reached for each other through the bars to embrace.

"This is my father," Billy said. "He killed the one who hurt me." His voice had softened and he no longer seemed rough or mean.

"Why are you locked up, sir?" Carlito asked. He was overcome with pity. Would it have been worse, he wondered, to see Papá suffer like this than to see him dead?

Realizing Carlito's distress, the man touched his arm tenderly. "Don't worry about me, lad. I did what was right."

Billy set the lantern on the damp floor. "We are from Cape Town," he began, "the English settlement there. Many months ago Father was shanghaied. I knew he'd been taken to the *Argentina* so I snuck aboard to find him. When we'd been at sea eight days an officer caught me and tried to throw me overboard, but Father stopped him. There was a terrible fight with swords.

"Unfortunately the officer he killed was Parvo's brother. Parvo is keeping us alive just to torment us, like a cat playing with its mouse. He plans to kill us eventually."

"There, there," said his father. "I'd do it all over again, Billy, I would."

A lantern in the distance revealed a man limping toward them, his wooden leg kicking at the rats. It was Simeon. He carried in his other hand a small pail of soup and a chunk of bread, which he slipped through the bars.

Mr. Bumpus took a quick gulp. He looked at Carlito.

"Here, lad," he said, offering the pail. "You are hungry. Please take some."

Carlito was embarrassed, but he took the pail and allowed himself one sip. How good the warm broth tasted. How good of this man to share with him, a stranger.

"Thank you, sir."

Simeon pulled two pieces of hardtack from his pocket and handed one to each boy. The biscuits were rock hard and had dark, moving spots. Carlito soon realized those spots were the heads of maggots.

"Like this, matey." Simeon took his biscuit and smacked it on the floor, knocking off two spots. "Eat the rest, they won't hurt you. Come dinner I'll give you a pot of tea for dipping. The bugs swim to the surface, you'll see. Now go along, mate, the captain's looking for you. Take my lamp."

When Carlito reached the companionway, he looked out to a blue sky. After being in darkness the sunlight made him squint.

They were less than a mile from shore, which was green with pine and twisted cypress; beyond were redwood forests with rivers that flowed to the sea. A waterfall cascaded fifty feet into the ocean, beautiful as a lace veil. From among the bluffs several spouts of steam rose in the cold air. Carlito knew these were the natural hot pools of the Esselen Indians, which were sometimes shared with Costanoans.

"You there!"

Carlito jumped. Captain Bouchard waved his arm at the shoreline, then made a fist. "This is not a sightseeing holiday, Spaniard. The next time you keep me waiting you'll be whipped. Stand at attention. . . . That's better."

The captain lowered his plump chin to look down at Carlito. "We will be landing shortly," he said. "You are to stay on the beach and guard my gig while I attend to business at Refugio Ranch. Is that clear?"

"Yes, sir."

Carlito knew the captain was testing him. Rancho de Refugio was owned by Señor Ortega, a friend of his family's and a fellow Spaniard. He felt sick knowing there would be trouble.

14
Refugio Beach
La playa del Refugio

Three boats from the *Argentina* and three from the *Santa Rosa* surfed into the narrow beach at Refugio. Two older boys joined Carlito and Billy Bumpus, as did a nine-year-old named Little Edward. His yellow hair was curly with bits of straw, and his hands were stained black, for he was one of the powder monkeys who carried gunpowder to the cannons.

He sat in the wet sand and began pulling off his boots. "Come on, mates, let's have ourselves a swim."

Carlito watched the path Bouchard had taken into the brush. Two dozen men had marched with him, sabers and guns ready. He'd been ordered to guard the boats, but for how long, he wondered? Even though the air was cool, the sunshine felt hot through his clothes, and the waves were such an inviting color, light green.

What harm would there be in a quick swim? It might be hours before Bouchard returned. Carlito looked again at the path, then kicked off his shoes. When he felt the warm sand between his toes this made him so happy he peeled off his shirt and pants, then threw them in the air as the other boys were doing.

A wave crested. Carlito ran toward it, dove under its foam, then came up sputtering. The water was so cold his ears hurt. Again and again the five boys dove and jumped and chased each other. They clanked the oars together as if sword fighting. They splashed through tide pools below the rocky bluffs, their shrieks and laughter heard by those watching from the ships.

From a mile inland came the cracks of gunfire. Carlito saw smoke. "Hurry," he called to the boys. They ran to find their clothes, but to pull sandy shirts and trousers over wet skin took a long time. They were still barefoot when the first pirate appeared running from the trees. He wore a red cap and waved a knife. His other arm held a small wooden chest.

"Varmints!" he yelled. "Why aren't the boats ready?" He shoved one of the older boys into the water and kicked sand into the other's face. "Collect the oars now or I'll have you shot."

By the time the crafts were launched into the surf Carlito heard what happened. Bouchard had looted the ranch before setting it on fire, but was then ambushed by *vaqueros* who captured three pirates with lassoes. He was now so enraged he sliced at the water with his sword, swearing oaths so vile his men were silenced.

As he pulled himself up the ship's ladder he yelled, "Navigator!"

"Sir!"

"Chart us to one of those islands where there'll be no whimpering Spaniards to bother us. Fools." He slapped his sword against the rail then disappeared down the companionway.

Immediately the sailor in the red cap grabbed Carlito and Little Edward by the arms and dragged them across the deck. As the boys struggled he lashed their wrists to an overhead ratline and pulled out a whip that had been soaking in a bucket of salt water.

"You'll never disobey my orders again, do you hear?"

Carlito squeezed his eyes shut in terror. He could hear Little Edward crying. There was a whistling sound from the lash, but it stopped midair. Carlito held his breath. There was a scuffle behind him, and cursing. He turned his head and stared in disbelief.

The pirate was being wrestled down by a woman. A large woman with wild yellow hair. Carlito had seen her before, but had not realized she was part of the crew.

She twisted his arm and tossed the whip overboard. "You ever lay another hand on these boys, I'll slice your ears off. Johnson, cut them down."

"Aye, Monty."

The woman stared at Red Cap until he looked away in submission, then she shoved him into a pile of ropes. The men watching were silent. Only the flap of sails announced they were once again at sea.

15
A Fresh Grave

Una sepultura nueva

Santa Cruz Island lay twenty-five miles southwest of Refugio Beach, a purple bump on the horizon between the smaller Anacapa and Santa Rosa islands. As night fell, Montague worked by lantern, studying her charts.

Sailing under a light breeze and pale moon, it was nearly dawn when the ships dropped anchor in a bay on the island's north side. Carlito was dozing below deck, curled in a nest of rope, when Billy Bumpus shook him awake.

"Captain says we're to hurry. No, leave your shoes here. Come, friend." Ever since Billy learned that Carlito's father had been murdered, he had treated Carlito with kindness.

Four boats from each ship were lowered. The boys stepped backward out the gangway, down the ladder into a yawl just as two sailors began rowing. Parvo was there, fingering his new gold necklace. His hair looked crimson in the early light and he leaned forward to scowl at them better. He reeked of rum.

"This island's deserted, lads, so don't look for natives to help you write home, heh-heh. Make sure you stay on firewood detail or I'll chain y'both to that rock and let the tide drown you. Out of my sight, now go!"

Billy and Carlito jumped over the gunwale into icy, waist-deep water. A swell immediately rose over their heads, so they frantically tried to swim, their wet clothes dragging them down. When the swell receded, their feet once again found bottom. They pulled with their arms. The next wave came only to their shoulders and pushed them gently toward the beach.

They could still hear Parvo's drunken laugh.

Shivering, the boys took off their shirts to wring them out. Carlito noticed that someone watched them from the *Argentina*'s quarterdeck. It was the woman. She was dressed like a sailor, but her hair blew around her face, free from tar.

"Who is she?" he asked.

Billy squeezed water out of his patch before tying it back on. "That's Montague," he said. "When we finally found the Sandwich Islands, half the crew had died from scurvy, including five officers and the navigator. Bouchard has such poor eyesight he needed to find someone to help him chart.

"He hates Montague, but she was the only navigator in the islands willing to come aboard this stinking ship. She brought California maps with her, drawn long ago by Cabrillo and Vizcaino. Bouchard needed her and he needed those maps."

Carlito pulled his wet shirt down over his head, but when he looked at the ship the woman had disappeared. He hoped to see her again, to thank her for rescuing him from the whip.

The sand was so cold their feet ached and their wet shirts made them feel chilled. They hurried up the beach to begin gathering wood. Sailors spread out in different directions, some with axes to cut trees, while others rolled barrels to the freshwater streams.

Carlito felt nervous when he saw the abandoned huts of the Chumash Indians, their blackened firepits. Families had lived here. He remembered the devastating earthquake of 1812, when he was five years old, and how terrified Indians had canoed across the channel to seek safety at the missions. Many of the survivors later died from a measles epidemic.

Had anyone been left behind? he wondered.

He and Billy filled their arms with kindling as they explored among the oaks. Carlito noticed that on the other side of a creek was a mound of fresh dirt the length of a child. On it shells were arranged in a type of decoration with a strand of blue beads. There were fresh footprints on the path.

The boys were surprised by a quick rustle in the shrubs, then the sound of someone running away.

"Who's there?" Carlito called. He dropped his wood

and started to follow, but Billy grabbed his arm.

"Stay with me, Spaniard."

"But someone lives on this island after all. They could help us hide until the ships leave. Come on."

Billy glanced toward the beach. "If Parvo finds me gone, he'll kill my father immediately, he told me he would. And if Parvo finds you gone, he'll punish me something terrible."

Carlito's throat felt tight. He was remembering that Parvo was the man who had killed his father and he suddenly wanted to protect Billy. He nodded slowly.

"*Amigo*, I understand."

16
A Visit to the Navigator

Una visita al navegante

The *Argentina* and *Santa Rosa* remained anchored in the island's wide bay for three nights. Carlito was homesick. His stomach ached with hunger. Because his clothes were sticky and damp from salt water, he constantly felt cold. He was so nervous about what the pirates might do to him, he had trouble sleeping.

On the main deck he lay inside a lifeboat that was being used as a chicken coop. It was snug, out of the wind. He gazed at stars and listened to the waves wash over the cobble beach, but the familiar barking of seals only sharpened his loneliness. How desperately he wanted to return home. He needed Mamá to comfort him over the loss of Papá.

During the day men scooped water from the streams into barrels, later rolling them down to the waves where they could be floated out to the ships.

The hills were thick with oak, pine, and manzanita, which were cut for firewood. Nearby was a cave. Here Parvo supervised the burial of three wooden chests. They were so heavy with coins and jewels it took nine men to drag them up through the sand. Here the treasure would be safe should the Spaniards capture the ships.

As Carlito gathered kindling he could smell mint along the creeks and the sweet aroma of lilacs and tiny wild roses. He studied footprints in the brush. There seemed to be several Chumash watching the pirates' activities from secret places. He wanted to make friends with these Indians, but he had promised Billy Bumpus he would stay close to shore and wouldn't try to escape, at least not now.

Late afternoon on the third day, the last barrels were hauled aboard. As the boys were rowed back to the ship, Carlito leaned over the side to look down at the clear, blue water. Forests of kelp swayed in the current, their roots anchored in the sand thirty feet below. Among their stalks swam garibaldi the color of bright oranges.

Where the bottom dropped away to a deeper blue, Carlito was startled to see a manta ray appear from beneath the boat. Its black wings, nearly ten feet across, moved gracefully up and down, its tail as long as a whip. He had heard sailors describe rays they'd seen off the coast of Baja California, giant ones with wingspans of twenty feet. They were supposedly as gentle as *las mariposas*.

Soon all was ready and the ships sailed into the channel. Dolphins swam alongside, as if happy to escort the pirates away from their beautiful island. The sky was busy with seagulls. Offshore, dignified brown pelicans soared inches above the swells without causing a ripple.

After sunset, campfires on the mainland began to appear, glowing like tiny, faraway eyes. Carlito went below to get warm and to look for something to eat. He found Simeon in the galley ladling soup. A silver bracelet above his elbow was from the spoils of Refugio Ranch, and tied into the braids of his beard were blue silk ribbons.

"Ho, laddie," he said. "Monty's looking for you. Her chart room is aft, below Parvo's quarters. Take her this." He handed him a thick pork sandwich wrapped in cloth, with a pail of tea. He then tucked Carlito's supper, a wedge of moldy cheese, into his shirt pocket. Its rancid smell made him cough, but Carlito was so starved he quickly ate it.

"And, laddie, don't spill or you'll make her mad."

"Aye, Simeon."

Carlito carried Montague's dinner, careful not to slosh her tea onto the swaying deck. As he hurried by the capstan, soldiers playing cards stopped to stare at him. He hurried between rows of hammocks and past an alcove where four sailors quietly mended clothes by lantern light. The air stunk with body odor and rat droppings.

Billy Bumpus came down the companionway with his

club. "Time to catch me some vermin." His grin moved his patch upward. He cheerfully punched Carlito on the shoulder as they passed each other. Down six steps, around a corner, down two more. Carlito stopped in front of a door with a brass plate that read *Navigator*. When he heard fierce arguing from inside, he backed into the shadows.

Suddenly the door banged open. Parvo stormed out, but not before Montague grabbed the front of his shirt and twisted it in her fist.

"Stay away from my maps, you spy, you little piece of bait."

"Hands off, woman."

"Oh?" She leaned into his face. "Bouchard would slit your throat if he knew of your plan to take over the ship — you'll not learn these charts as long as I'm around." She flung Parvo into the hallway.

His face was dark with rage as he straightened his shirt. "You'll pay for this."

"Parvo, you're scum." She spat on his long red hair before slamming the door.

Carlito's knees felt weak. He waited. When Parvo's angry steps faded, he shyly knocked by the nameplate.

"What."

"It's your supper, miss."

She unhooked the latch. Her large body filled the doorway. "Come in," she said.

In the light Carlito saw her face for the first time. She looked young, perhaps twenty years old. Her cheeks, nose, and forehead were covered with smallpox scars, like thumbprints. Carlito felt scared by her lack of beauty until he looked into her eyes. They were a gentle blue.

Her window was propped open. In came the sound of splashing, for directly below was the ship's wake, swirling in the darkness. Wind rustled papers on her desk. There was the pleasant aroma of kerosene and damp hemp. She motioned to a small table set for two, with pewter plates and cups.

"Sit down, little Spaniard. I've been waiting for you."

17
Santa Barbara

Santa Bárbara

From her belt she unsheathed her knife and cut the sandwich in two, setting one half on each plate. She poured tea into their cups and pointed for him to eat. Famished, Carlito shoved the meat and bread into his mouth.

After watching him for a moment she said, "You want off this ship, yes?"

For some reason Carlito trusted her. Her kindness made him think of his mother. He nodded, trying not to cry. "I want to go home," he whispered.

She appeared in thought, chewing slowly. Her tongue moved food to the side of her mouth, then she reached in to yank at something bothering her. Out came a black tooth. She examined it for a moment before tossing it out the window.

"Manoverboard, manoverboard!" shrieked a voice from a corner of the room. Carlito flinched. He hadn't noticed the parrot. It perched in a bamboo cage, bobbing nervously. Its belly was bright yellow, its wings turquoise.

"It's all right, Mr. Biscuit," the woman said. As she gently stroked his neck with her finger, he closed his eyes. The lids were black-and-white stripes. Carlito had never seen such a beautiful bird.

"Spaniard," she continued, "we will be landing soon at Santa Barbara. Your governor most likely will be there looking for you and for his three men imprisoned aboard the *Santa Rosa*. That means Bouchard will watch you closely. Do not disobey him or he will hurt you. I might have a way to sneak you ashore."

She rolled up her sleeves, revealing muscular arms with tattoos: a lion on one, a parrot on the other, drawn between pox scars. Her calloused hands enfolded Carlito's. "Mention our talk to no one. No one. When you find Little Edward and Billy, tell them to come see Monty. Tonight."

The pirates anchored at sunrise, seven days after leaving Monterey in flames. While Carlito scrubbed Bouchard's privy, he looked out the salt-encrusted windows at Santa Barbara. He hoped Montague was right, that his friend Governor Solá was waiting.

A wide sandy beach curved at the bay's edge. Hills surrounded the village of adobes and dusty streets. In the distance was the mission. Recently repaired from earthquake damage, its white buildings were a landmark for ships at sea. Bells rang from twin towers, warning of the intruders.

Bouchard stood on deck with his spyglass. Sailors rowed Peter Corney to the *Argentina* so the two captains could talk. They decided to send a letter to shore with Lieutenant Woodburn and thirty soldiers, demanding a prisoner exchange. Carlito felt jubilant thinking he might be freed. He and Governor Solá would ride north along the Royal Highway, back to his beloved mother and sister.

Carlito watched as two cutters and the yawl tried to surf the rough waves. One of the boats turned sideways in the swell, then rolled over, dumping everyone into the water. There was much commotion as the men struggled to grab oars and swim in their heavy clothes to shore. When it was discovered that two officers had drowned, Bouchard became enraged. He cursed through his tin horn for all to hear.

He cursed again when he saw horsemen with muskets. It appeared there were hundreds ready to shoot, but it was only a small army marching in circles around a hill trying to fool the pirates.

Bouchard yelled in Spanish, "Worms! Give me back my men now or there'll be nothing left of your pathetic city." He raised his arm and three cannons fired. The noise rattled the windows and hurt Carlito's ears. Explosions at the high-water mark sprayed sand ninety feet into the air.

Two Spaniards on stallions galloped along the beach carrying a white flag of surrender. An hour later the *Santa Rosa*'s three prisoners were led up to the deck and their handcuffs removed. They waited for the shore boat. Aboard were three scowling pirates captured at Refugio Ranch who had been chained up in Santa Barbara's hoosegow.

When Carlito realized the prisoner exchange did not include him, he slumped to the cabin floor in despair. He kicked the bucket of water, spilling suds under the swinging bed. He'd forgotten Bouchard did not consider him a prisoner. Another thought upset him.

Perhaps Governor Solá had no idea he was aboard the black frigate. If Ziba and Pedro had drowned that night, then people would assume he had, too.

Carlito was heartsick. His family didn't know where he was.

18
Heading South

Rumbo al sur

Carlito mopped under the captain's table and straightened the bedsheets. He felt hopeless when he heard the bo's'n's whistle and the creak of ropes as sails worked to catch the wind. Where were the ships going now, he wondered, and what was Montague's plan?

He found her in the galley eating a slab of ham over bread. Simeon sat next to her, his wooden leg on his lap as he carved a new design with his knife. Simeon's stump was visible through the end of a short trouser. It was swollen and coated with tar.

"It's been nearly three months, laddie," he said in response to Carlito's stare. "Boiling tar's what stopped the bleeding."

"But how . . . ?"

"Shark. Was painting the side of the ship, lad, sitting on a sling beneath the bow. My feet were skimming the water and the shark came right at me, biggest white I've ever seen. Monty here, she was keeping an eye and pulled me up before any of the mates knew what happened. Surgeon dipped what was left of my knee into his bucket of tar and there you have it."

Simeon rolled the wood to show Carlito an engraved parrot with striped eyelids like Mr. Biscuit's. Next to it was a woman with long tresses; she had Monty's face, but without scars. Farther down was a one-eyed boy with a patch, and a smaller boy.

"Little Edward?" pointed Carlito.

"Yes," said Simeon. "This is where I keep my friends, that way they'll never leave me. Hungry?"

"Yes, Simeon, I am."

"There's a good lad." He passed him a steaming cup of soup. It was thick with beans and chunks of ham. "Go along now. Captain hates to see boys enjoying themselves."

As the *Argentina* and *Santa Rosa* sailed down the coast, the islands of Santa Cruz and Anacapa remained lumps on the horizon. Just before sunset they approached the point of land where Mission San Buenaventura stood, finally rebuilt after being destroyed in the 1812 earthquake. A tidal wave then had forced the padres and Indians to flee to the hills, which was where they now hid. Fields and orchards were deserted, the tower bells silent.

Bouchard looked through his glass. A tassel on his bicorn hat ruffled in the wind. "Fools," he laughed. "They all run scared from Hippolyte de Bouchard, ha-ha." He raised his arm. Two guns thundered. Cannonballs carved craters on the beach, but did the village no harm.

When night fell, Carlito, Billy, and Little Edward covered themselves with a sheet of canvas and lay under one of the cutters that was stored upside down on the main deck. The breeze had stopped. Now the ship rolled heavily in the swell, back and forth, which made the boys feel sick. Without wind, the frigate was tossed like a piece of bark.

Stars reflected off the quiet sea, making it impossible to tell where sky met water. Every half hour the ship's bell rang to mark time, and every four hours to mark the changing of the watch. Carlito tried to sleep.

He heard the murmur of voices from the forecastle, which was directly below. Feet shuffled to a jig being played on a fife. The ship groaned as ropes rubbed against wood, and there was sloshing as waves hit the hull. He lay quietly, aware of a new sound, a soft *whooosh*.

He crawled out from under the boat to listen. There it was again, on the water, not too far away. *Whooosh*. He strained to see through the darkness. Someone came beside him. It was Montague. Her golden hair blew around her face. In the darkness her skin looked smooth and Carlito thought her beautiful. Is this how Simeon saw her?

"Whales are out there, little Spaniard, you'll see them tomorrow." She took his hand and folded his fingers around something soft. It was a cluster of figs. She pointed to Billy and Little Edward curled together under the boat.

"Share these, then give them this warning: Parvo is scheming to get rid of you boys. Beware." She steadied herself against the swaying mast, then climbed down the companionway.

19
"Man Overboard!"

"¡Hombre al agua!"

For five days the ships rolled in the swell, no wind to fill their sails. They drifted south with a current that kept them dangerously near the surf.

Montague watched the sea. More islands lay on the horizon: San Nicolas; Santa Barbara; and further south, Santa Catalina. At noon every day she measured the sun's height with her sextant to calculate how far they'd come.

Bouchard paced the deck. "Montague," he said to her back, "we are too close to shore and it's your fault. All it will take for us to be pushed onto the rocks is a few strong waves. How dare you not salute when I address you?"

Slowly she turned toward him, the sextant cradled in her arm. In the sunlight the pox scars on her face looked deep. She was six-foot-two, eight inches taller than the captain.

"Sir," she began. "When the storm off Kauai nearly sunk this floating piece of excrement, you blamed me.

When the Spaniards' guns killed seven of your buffoons, you blamed me. Now God chooses to send no wind, and you blame me again.

"Perhaps, Captain Bouchard, your poor luck is due more to the nature of your petty, vile business, than it is my navigational skills, which may I remind you, far surpass anything you'll ever comprehend. Sir."

Bouchard drew in a deep breath. His face was red. He clamped his shaking hands behind his back. Through clenched teeth he said, "And may I remind *you*, madame, that you are speaking to the captain of this vessel and I could put you in chains, then have you court-martialed when we reach Buenos Aires. What are you pig farmers staring at?" he yelled to the gathering men. Quickly they turned away.

Parvo came to his side. His hair was greased back and fell behind his shoulders like a dark red hood. His mouth drew up in a cruel smile. "I say we tie her arms behind her and let her swim. Sir, everyone knows women are bad luck at sea, especially those with the face of a dog and a big . . ."

He didn't get to finish. Montague passed the sextant to Little Edward and stepped up to Parvo. She grabbed his shoulders and lifted him in her strong arms. One boot slipped off as he tried to kick her. She carried him toward the rail and, before anyone could stop her, heaved him into the ocean.

"Man overboard!" someone cried. The ship's bell clanged wildly. Sailors crowded the side to peer down at Parvo splashing and trying to curse through mouthfuls of salt water. Silently Carlito cheered. How he hated this murderer and hoped he would be grabbed by a shark.

Within thirty seconds the pinnace was lowered with two men rowing. They reached Parvo and pulled at his soaking shirt and pants until he was in. His remaining boot floated for a moment before filling with water and sinking. Had there been wind, he would have drowned before help arrived.

Bouchard narrowed his eyes at Montague. "This is gross insubordination," he said, "and you will be punished."

20
Bouchard's Dilemma
El problema de Bouchard

Carlito carefully carried the heavy tray to Bouchard's cabin. On it were two roast chickens, steaming biscuits, and a pot of tea. He was so hungry, he licked the meat before tapping the door with his foot.

When it was opened, he stepped over the six-inch high threshold, then walked to the long table where he arranged the food.

At one end sat Bouchard. Parvo and two other officers leaned over the map in front of him, arguing.

". . . but if you kill her, who will chart us back to Santa Cruz Island? My shares of doubloons are still buried there."

Carlito stiffened every time he saw Parvo. He recognized one of the other men as the surgeon. He wore a powdered wig that curled above his ears. Quite fat, his chin wobbled as he spoke. He reached for the chicken, twisted off one of the crispy legs, and bit it.

Grease dripped from his lips. "Another thing," he said, chewing with his mouth open, "if we lock 'er up in the brig with that other traitor she'll not have the sun or stars to mark our route."

Bouchard looked out the windows at the rolling sea, then studied his hands. One of his rings was a large square emerald, which he rubbed with his finger. "Parvo," he said after a moment.

"Sir?"

"If you were master of this ship, what would you do if you discovered a traitor aboard, someone who would not serve you loyally? Tell me."

Parvo glanced at Carlito, but was so flattered to have been asked his opinion he didn't want to interrupt the moment by making the boy leave.

"Sir, you are wise to consider these things," Parvo began. He leaned back in his chair, arms behind his head. "I would maroon the traitor. These islands are deserted, plus there're at least two with no water. Montague herself told me about Anacapa and Dead Man's Island. Sir."

Bouchard was thoughtful. He motioned for Carlito to pour his tea. "Continue, Mr. Parvo," he said.

"There's a lad on the *Santa Rosa.* Sir. Corney's been teaching him navigation. We could bring him aboard and make sure he can manage the sextant before ridding ourselves of that foul woman. In the meantime, keep the dog in her quarters. Sir."

The surgeon licked his fingers. Still chewing he said,

"But why maroon someone instead of making a quick end of them under the keel?"

"Because, Mr. Surgeon, that would be too kind. A slow death without a drop of water to drink is what traitors deserve."

Captain Bouchard smiled. "Well done, Mr. Parvo." He waved at Carlito to open the door. "Thank you, gentlemen. That will be all."

21
San Juan Capistrano
San Juan Capistrano

Carlito's hatred for Parvo increased when he heard the plot against Montague. He didn't want her to die. Not only had she comforted him and been kind, she was the only one who seemed willing to help him escape.

She was calm when he told her. "I've always known my days here were numbered; at least I'll be off this cursed vessel," she said, leaning out the window to rest her chin on her arm. Wind blew her hair off her neck, revealing scars the size of buttons.

"But you might never get off alive," whispered Carlito. His forehead hurt from trying not to cry.

"On a deserted island, little Spaniard, it will no longer matter that I'm ugly. Do you know what a relief that'll be? My only regret is that I won't be here to help you and the other boys."

* * *

Finally wind rose out of the west. As the ships sailed south past Santa Monica, cannons were fired at soldiers standing on the dunes.

The pirates passed the wide sandy beaches of Redondo where salt was harvested, then rounded Point Fermin to San Pedro Bay. There were adobe huts near shore, but no soldiers. Here a road led through vineyards and fields of grazing cattle to Pueblo Los Angeles twenty miles away.

At the mouth of the harbor was *La Isla del Muerto*, Dead Man's Island. Its sides sloped thirty-five feet up to a barren plateau. The water rippled with sharks.

Parvo and Bouchard stood on the windy quarterdeck.

"There, sir. Shall we stop now and escort the lady ashore?"

"Not yet, Mr. Parvo. Patience."

From the sea, Mission San Juan Capistrano looked like a shining block of white. It sat on a quiet, green hill, its church still in ruins from the big quake. To the northeast were mountains: the rugged, snowcapped San Gabriels.

The ships anchored in a cove facing sandstone cliffs that rose like a wall above the beach. It was the cool, sunny morning of December 14, 1818.

A Californian on horseback waited onshore for the pirates to lower boats. Finally Lieutenant Woodburn stepped out of his launch into shallow water and walked up the pebbly beach.

"Who are you?" demanded the lieutenant. His voice carried across the water to those watching from aboard ship.

"I am Alférez Santiago Argüello," the man said, shifting in his saddle better to hold the flag of Spain. "I have with me the army from Presidio San Diego, and our message to you is 'Go away.' "

Lieutenant Woodburn laughed. He stroked the horse's braided halter. "And our message to you, Señor Argüello, is this: Captain Bouchard wants powder, shot, and fresh meat. If you oblige, he will spare San Juan Capistrano."

Señor Argüello looked up the steep path. High above, horsemen paced. "If you choose to land," he responded, "we most certainly will provide you with powder and shot, more than you'll ever need."

When Lieutenant Woodburn delivered this message to the *Argentina*, Bouchard threw his hat to the deck. "How dare he be so impudent! Men, to shore!"

At the sight of pirates swarming off the ships Argüello retreated. He and his army galloped east to warn the villagers.

Carlito leaned out one of the empty gun ports to watch the boats land. Three cannons were being pulled by ropes up to the bluff where they could aim at the mission. He was sad there would be another battle. He closed his eyes and breathed in the pleasant scent of wood and tar and salt air, pretending for a moment that he was home. Was Mamá all right? Would he ever see his family again?

He felt weary and hungry. He was exhausted from lack of sleep. The damp air kept Carlito's clothes from drying, which rubbed his skin raw. Sores had developed under his arms and on the inside of his legs so that it hurt to walk. A splinter under his toe had gone so deep, the wound was now infected.

Even if he could escape, would he be able to run?

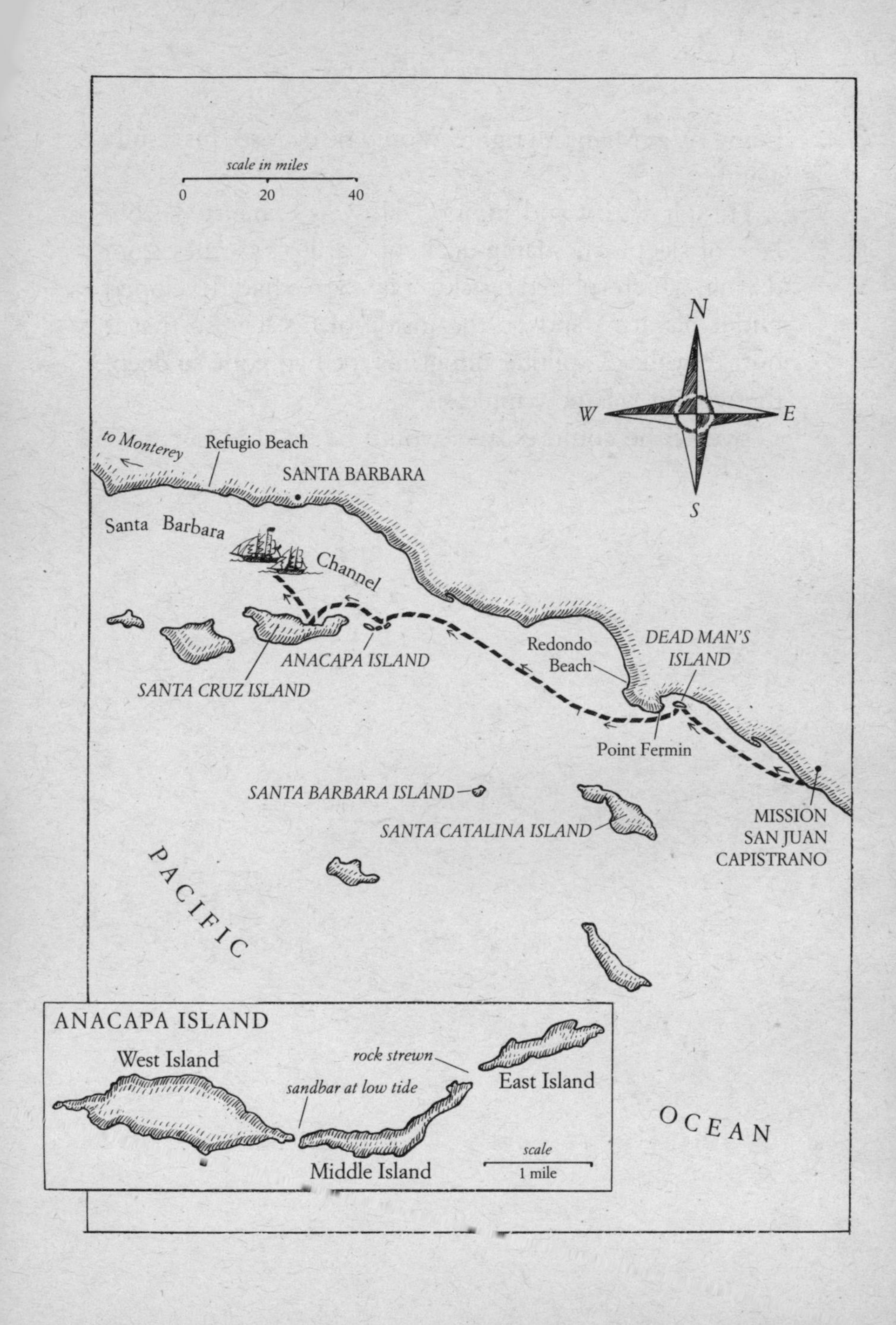
scale in miles
0
20
40
N
W
E
S
to Monterey
Refugio Beach
SANTA BARBARA
Santa Barbara Channel
ANACAPA ISLAND
SANTA CRUZ ISLAND
Redondo Beach
DEAD MAN'S ISLAND
Point Fermin
SANTA BARBARA ISLAND
SANTA CATALINA ISLAND
MISSION SAN JUAN CAPISTRANO
PACIFIC
OCEAN
ANACAPA ISLAND
West Island
rock strewn
East Island
sandbar at low tide
Middle Island
scale
1 mile

22
Montague's Story
La historia de Montague

Five older boys were ordered to stand guard on the beach under punishment of hanging if they were caught swimming or leaving the boats unattended.

All morning Carlito listened to gunshots and cannons. There was laughter and drunken shouts. Since he, Billy, and Little Edward were the only ones allowed to visit Montague, who was confined to her quarters, Simeon prepared a meal for them to take her.

"Give this to Mr. Biscuit," he said of the hardtack he set on the tray, "and here's a little something for Red Cap." Simeon licked the end of a cork, then squeezed it down into a jug that he had filled with rum. "And lads . . . tell Monty I miss her. Tell her it's the captain that won't let me see 'er."

Her door was guarded by the pirate in the red cap. Hate was in his eyes until Little Edward offered the jug.

"Give it," he said, pulling it to his chest. He wiggled out the cork and sniffed. "Ah, laddies, this suits me fine. Now get in there but don't try any tricks."

Red Cap flipped a dagger out of his boot and touched its tip to Carlito's throat, then Billy's, then Little Edward's. "That's right, mateys, we'll swab the deck with your blood if you make a false move." He kicked the door open, then when the boys ducked inside, closed it with a slam.

Montague sat at her desk writing in a log book. Sunlight filled the small room and through the opened window came a cool breeze. There was a view of the bay, then the cliffs and beach as the *Argentina* drifted around its anchor.

When she smiled at them, Carlito noticed another tooth missing. She set out the slab of pork they'd brought and cut it into four parts. She did the same to the cheese and loaf of bread. "Eat, boys," she said. "Mr. Biscuit, look what our friends brought. Can you say thank you?"

"Manoverboard." The parrot lifted his foot to climb on her finger. He stretched his neck to look at the boys. "Manoverboard," he squawked again. She set him on the table where he found the hardtack, picked it up with his beak, then waddled over to the window seat. There he pecked at the head of a maggot.

"Monty, what's this?" Carlito asked after he'd eaten. He held a fuzzy cannonball that had been inside a basket filled with exotic shells.

"Coconut, from the Sandwich Islands. You'll not see a more lovely place on earth."

"Then why did you leave?"

She was quiet for a moment. A gust of wind ruffled the parrot's feathers. "Lads, take a seat," she said softly. She sat on the floor, arms wrapped around her thick knees.

"My father was captain of the brig *Evergreen*, out of London. He taught me about the sea, how to navigate. His first mate was Jack Monday, a handsome fellow; oh, how sharp he looked in his uniform. I was fifteen when we became sweethearts, sixteen when we decided to marry."

Montague poured tea into her cup, took a sip then nodded for the boys to pass it around. The sounds of gunfire continued to echo across the bay.

"We were in Honolulu," she continued, "repairing our mainmast when the islands were hit with an epidemic: smallpox. I was the unlucky one in my family, because I survived. My three little sisters, mother and father, they all threw themselves into the sea, so terrible was their fever. My dear Jack nursed me back to health, laddies. He was so good to me. We talked about the cottage we'd have, the roses. We even picked names for our babies.

"But one day he could no longer bear to look at the scars on my face. Jack Monday packed his sea chest and sailed back to England without me."

She stroked Mr. Biscuit's bright blue head. When Little Edward reached over to touch her arm, she put her hand on his and smiled sadly. "Yes, I was heartbroken. For three years I lived with a merchant and his wife who treated me like a slave.

"When Captain Bouchard came along with stories of adventure, well, boys, I easily fell under his spell. He needed a navigator. I needed freedom. He would give me my own quarters, food, part of his treasures . . ."

"But why does he hate you so much?" asked Billy.

"He hates me because I'm not afraid of him. And because . . ." Suddenly she held her hand up for silence. There was a rough sound outside her door.

She whispered, "Red Cap has promised to kill you boys. Now I have a job to do. Stand aside, lads."

23
The Floggings
Los azotes

Red Cap was too drunk to know he was being dragged, then lifted, then rolled out the window. Down he went like a stone. His arms and legs flew up in a splash.

Carlito watched the man struggle for a moment, hoping he would swim for shore, but suddenly he sank, his cap drifting slowly down after him. Again and again Mr. Biscuit cried, "Manoverboard . . ." Carlito was shocked that Montague had so easily sent a man to his death. Most of all he was horrified that he, an honorable Spaniard, hadn't tried to stop her. It happened so quickly.

Had it been Parvo, though, yes, he would have given the first shove.

Little Edward looked surprised, as if he'd just witnessed his first crime, but not Billy. He shook his fist in the air. "That piece of scum beat me and my father for no reason time and time again. Good riddance."

* * *

Bouchard's victory band marched on the bluff, led by men carrying flags: one blue and white for Argentina, the other one black with a skull.

Late afternoon, however, cries from the cliff could be heard as pirates began stumbling down the path. Some were so drunk their mates dragged them by their hair along the rocky beach.

Bouchard paced the deck. He was humiliated that José de la Guerra had ridden from Santa Barbara with his small army to join Señor Argüello's. He was once again enraged to hear that some of his crew had been captured.

His temper increased when it became obvious that, instead of looking for gold or gunpowder, the men had raided *aguardiente*, the fiery home-brewed whiskey hidden in an underground *bodega*.

"They'll be flogged at sunrise, when they've sobered up enough to feel it!" Bouchard stabbed the air with his cutlass, cursing so loudly that spit flew from his mouth. Not until he saw the two Indian girls did his temper soften. They were slung over the shoulders of pirates climbing the ladder to the gangway.

"Well done, gentlemen," he said with a nod toward the frightened girls, "well done."

Once again anchors were raised and the *Argentina* and *Santa Rosa* slipped out of the bay. Carlito looked down into the clear water. He saw on the sandy bottom a red dot and several feet away Red Cap's sprawled body. Even though he had hated the pirate, he was ashamed he had witnessed his murder. And he thought it sad no one seemed to notice or care that Red Cap had disappeared.

Now that a northerly course was set, the ships beat into the wind. The waves were rough and gray. As the sun dipped into the sea, night fell quickly. A cold wind rattled the halyards.

At sunrise the floggings began. All hands were ordered to stand at attention, including Montague, to witness the punishments; Bouchard wanted his crew to fear him. Over the next three hours twenty men were strung up, stripped to the waist, then bloodied with twelve lashes each.

Carlito was dizzy and he felt sick. He wanted to hide. For the first time he envied Billy's poor father being chained below. At least Mr. Bumpus couldn't hear the men's cries or smell their blood.

24
Dead Man's Island

La Isla del Muerto

The end came quickly for Montague. Her last words to Carlito were, "I'm sorry I couldn't help you, little Spaniard."

On December 17, after the new navigator boarded the *Argentina*, Montague was rowed to the narrow beach of *La Isla del Muerto*, a lonely island off San Pedro Bay. Parvo had insisted he take the oars himself and now he could not resist snickering with pleasure. Marooned with her were two soldiers who had spit in Bouchard's face after being flogged. Resigned to their terrible fate, they helped her ashore as if she were queen.

Billy Bumpus and Carlito stood at the railing with Little Edward, watching in silence. Simeon tried to console them, but his face was sad. He pressed two fingers to his lips, then held them in the air as if wind could carry his kiss to her.

Carlito would always remember Montague standing tall on the beach, her blond hair framing a face that from a distance looked beautiful. He wanted to cry out to her words of comfort. He wished he had thanked her for caring for him, but it was too late now.

Parvo rowed back to the *Argentina*. He was whistling a happy tune until he noticed the sharks. Five black fins were closing in on his little boat. In a panic he grabbed the ladder and clawed his way up to the deck. After brushing his coat off he laughed nervously. "Ha. The woman is doomed. If she tries to swim to shore those sharks will teach her a thing or two. Serves her right."

Carlito signaled Billy and Little Edward. They hurried down the companionway, then aft to Montague's quarters, but Captain Bouchard was already there. Out the window he was throwing the contents of her sea chest, her bedding, the basket of shells, the coconut. Her books fluttered down to the water like wounded birds.

In a fury he turned over her desk, then one by one heaved out the chairs and candles, her Bible and bottle of ink.

When he started to break apart her table, he saw the boys. "What are you babies staring at?" he roared. He kicked the wall before grabbing Mr. Biscuit's cage. He shoved past them out of the room, the parrot squawking in distress.

They waited until they heard Bouchard's steps overhead. "Let's hurry," Carlito said. Little Edward and Billy followed him to the lower deck where Carlito had first crawled aboard. The animal pen now had two sheep and one lamb. He pushed his foot through the straw until he found his knife and lariat.

"Let's get your father and jump this stinking ship," he said. Once again Carlito was a leader with careless plans, acting on wild impulse. Now that Parvo had cast off Montague, Carlito hated him even more. He hoped that by escaping he would somehow be able to alert a passing ship that would kill the pirates, rescue them and the two Indian girls, then sail back to Dead Man's Island to rescue Montague. There was no time to lose.

The boys took turns sawing at the wood below the brig, which was rotted by mold and urine. The stench made their eyes sting.

"Oh, laddies, I'm with ye, keep going," said Mr. Bumpus, his hands folded in prayer.

Carlito tied his rope to the loose bar and pulled while Billy chiseled at its base. Little Edward held the lantern. Its candle was only one-inch high and the flame was beginning to drown in the melting wax. "Hurry, hurry," he said.

Finally one of the iron bars popped free and Mr. Bumpus turned sideways to slip out.

But from the shadows a man coughed. The boys froze.

It was several moments before Carlito was able to speak. "Who goes there?" he whispered.

Out of the dark stepped Captain Bouchard. Next to him was Parvo, hands on hips.

In a low, even voice Bouchard said, "This is mutiny.

Punishable by death. Mr. Parvo, you choose the manner in which these vermin should die."

The ship was now in the rough waters of the channel. It rolled with the deep swells. The wood creaked. The lantern cast pale light as it swayed from Little Edward's hand. Rats scurried over their feet.

Parvo's face was in shadow, but there was no mistaking his sinister smile. "Maroon them. The old man, too. They're mutineers. Scum. Pig farmers. Get them off our ship."

"Thank you, Mr. Parvo. Tell our new navigator to find the latitude for Anacapa Island."

25
Marooned
Los abandonados

For eight days and nights Mr. Bumpus and the three boys were locked in Montague's cabin, the windows nailed shut. The lack of fresh air made them sick and the bucket they used for a chamber pot overflowed onto the floor where they tried to sleep.

They saw Santa Catalina Island pass behind them off the port side, California's barren coastline off the starboard. The ships made slow progress as they beat into the wind against strong currents.

The door was guarded by three Sandwich Islanders who, despite their size, didn't frighten Carlito the way Red Cap had. Before each sunset one loaf of bread was thrown in and a pail of drinking water set onto the soiled floor.

The smell made Carlito gag every time he took a sip of water. His throat was so sore it hurt to swallow, and his ankles were now raw with flea bites. He was miserable.

Little Edward clung to Billy's father. "There, there, laddies," the man often told them, "we'll be out of this filth soon enough." Though his beard and hair were crawling with lice, each boy sought comfort in his emaciated arms.

On the ninth morning the prisoners were led up to the deck. Low clouds hung over the sea, gray and cold. The frigate was anchored outside the kelp beds of Anacapa Island.

Carlito was surprised to see soldiers and sailors at attention. The Indian girls stood next to Captain Bouchard. Their cotton dresses were torn.

Parvo's hair was tied back in a pigtail with a black ribbon on its end. He seemed cheerful as he faced Mr. Bumpus and the boys. He sniffed at them, then held his nose dramatically.

"My, the stink of you foul creatures! But never mind. I have the honor of rowing you to your new home. By permission of our generous captain who, as you well know, adores children, and since it is Christmas morning, I am allowing you to take a few items to make your stay more pleasant."

He threw his head back with a single laugh, enjoying his humor. He swept his arm toward the cage holding Mr. Biscuit, and a crate that held a jug of water, a cabbage, an onion, and a live lamb.

"The victuals are for your dining pleasure." The more Parvo laughed, the more Carlito hated him. He tried to catch Simeon's eye, but the good man couldn't bear to look at his young friends.

"And let's not forget entertainment, ha-ha." He shoved the girls toward Mr. Bumpus. "We've no more use for them, and besides we all know perfectly well that women are bad luck at sea. Off you go, lassies." He prodded them with his boot.

One by one the six prisoners stepped to the gangway, then turned around to climb down the ladder. The lamb and parrot were put in the crate, then lowered by pulley into the boat. With a flourish Parvo took the oars and began to row. This time he insisted no crew accompany him.

He landed the cutter on the sandbar separating Anacapa's west end with its middle, for it was actually three little islands in a row. A herd of barking sea lions slid off the rocks into the waves. Mr. Bumpus helped the girls out, the boys carried the box and Mr. Biscuit. The lamb immediately began scaling the rocky cliff.

A sudden explosion splashed the shallow water. A puff of smoke rose above the *Argentina*'s stern. Terrified, Parvo fell backward into the surf while the others ran. The next explosion splintered the boat and sent gravel spitting into the air.

"What, what?" he screamed, waving his arms. "Hippolyte!"

Now it was Captain Bouchard who laughed. He stared at the castaways as his men put his ship to sea.

26
Isabella and Maria

Isabel y María

While Parvo yelled and begged Hippolyte to turn back, the others followed the lamb up to a bluff that rolled into a small valley protected from the wind. Though Anacapa had no fresh water, there was sagebrush, cactus, and flowers, unlike the island where Montague was.

The ocean spread in every direction, the mighty Pacific swells tipped with whitecaps. In the channel a pod of gray whales was swimming south, their spouts like tiny geysers.

When sunshine broke through the overcast, the sky turned brilliant blue. Carlito watched the ships round the point, then sail toward Santa Cruz Island five miles west. He hoped the pirates wouldn't discover that Chumash were hiding in the hills there.

Carlito lay on his stomach to peer down the cliff. Parvo sat on the beach where the rising tide washed over his legs. He punched the water with his fists and screamed, but his cries weren't heard over the wind and pounding surf. Carlito wanted to throw rocks at him, but he was interrupted by Billy's shouts.

"Free at last, we're free, and it's Christmas!" Billy and Little Edward had taken off their shirts and were waving them in the wind. Mr. Bumpus sat on a lichen-spotted rock, smiling, but too tired to shout.

When Carlito saw the girls sitting quietly by themselves, he went over to them. He wondered about their days aboard ship, but not wanting to embarrass them, didn't ask. To his surprise they answered his greeting in Spanish.

"My sister and I wish to clean ourselves," said Isabella, "then we will search for something to eat." She was fourteen, Maria twelve. They were both pretty with brown eyes and brown hair that fell to their shoulders.

Carlito was happy to once again speak his own language. He introduced them to the others, translating into English the plan to look for food.

Suddenly he realized their terrible predicament. This middle islet was small, one and a half miles long, a quarter of a mile wide, and they were at least fifteen miles from the mainland. It could be weeks before a friendly ship came near. Also, it was winter: They would need shelter and more than a jug of water to survive; their clothes were soiled and damp.

Carlito was most upset though, because Parvo was here, the man who killed his father and who had treated them so cruelly. Carlito wanted revenge.

A steep path was found leading down to a cove on the island's south side. A narrow crescent of beach met the water. Here the girls bathed. They rinsed out their dresses and dried their hair in the warm sunshine. After searching the tide pools they climbed back up the trail, their arms full. Carlito was amazed they had woven a basket from seaweed and filled it with small crabs, several sea cucumbers, a purple starfish, and an octopus, its head the size of a plum.

The girls laughed together as they arranged a meal for everyone, saving the onion and cabbage for another time.

"Our people camp here," said Isabella, "but only two days at a time, to rest between islands. See over there?" She pointed to a mound of shells bleached white from the sun. "Many abalone were eaten."

Maria gathered six of the large, bowl-shaped shells. Into each she portioned bits of raw octopus and the other sea creatures. Mr. Bumpus gathered them together in the grass to say a blessing, then he pulled out the cork on the jug and passed it around.

The brackish water made Carlito cough. He poured some into a shell for Mr. Biscuit, who for hours had sat silently in his cage, his striped eyes closed. Even when Edward offered a cricket he just captured, the parrot turned away.

Mr. Bumpus ate half his food, then set aside the rest.

"Aren't you hungry, Father?" asked Billy.

"We must feed Mr. Parvo."

Carlito picked up a rock and heaved it over the cliff. "Why?" he cried. "He's a murderer, my enemy. He deserves to die."

"Yes, laddie, I know. But we must hope that we will be rescued. I would rejoice to see your Governor Solá bring this evil man to justice. Besides, children, today is Christmas."

"I don't care about Christmas," yelled Carlito.

Several moments passed. Seagulls had begun circling overhead, ready to steal any leftovers. Billy gave Carlito a sympathetic look then said, "I'll go, Father." His shirt lay drying over a bush. He put it on, then retied his patch so it wouldn't slip down onto his cheek. He hurried away, disappearing over a ridge.

Carlito watched. Parvo still sat on the sandbar, the water now above his waist. When Billy offered the food and pointed up to the bluff, Parvo kicked the shell out of his hands.

The pirate wanted no part of Anacapa, but the rising tide would soon force him to swim or climb.

The sun set behind Santa Cruz Island. Its silhouette looked like a boy sleeping on his side. Carlito imagined the two ships were by now anchored in a snug cove. Captain Bouchard and Captain Corney were probably raising their goblets of wine in a victory toast, excited that they soon would be digging up their treasure.

27
The Cave
La caverna

Carlito woke to find himself curled among the five others in a grassy hollow, safe from the wind. He didn't remember falling asleep or even searching for shelter. Someone had woven brush into Mr. Biscuit's cage to keep him warm. The lamb lay between the girls.

Carlito's steps were wobbly as he searched for a place to relieve himself. After nearly four weeks at sea he felt dizzy to be on solid ground.

The morning air was cold. Fog hid the ocean and muffled the sound of waves. The closer he came to the cliff's edge, the louder was the barking of sea lions. He could smell salt and damp soil, pleasant smells because they reminded him of home.

For a moment he was confused. Was his father really dead, or was it all a bad dream? He glanced at his sleeping friends, their tattered clothes and thin arms covering each other. With a suddenness that surprised him, he fell to his knees with a sob.

Oh, Papá. Carlito cried from his heart, finally feeling the pain he'd been forced to put aside. *Papá, Papá . . .*

He felt something move close to him. It was the lamb. Its black face nuzzled Carlito's shoulder like a puppy, and Carlito responded by wrapping his arms around the woolly neck. He cried and cried while the lamb sat patiently.

When Carlito finally drew away, he noticed his sleeves were soaked. He gently grabbed a tuft of wool and twisted. Water dripped from the lamb's coat, so he tasted it. It was fresh, not salty. Carlito drank some more. How thirsty he'd been.

Now he knew why flowers and grass were able to grow here. Mist settled on the island at night, like a gentle rain.

If they kept the lamb alive instead of eating it, they would have fresh water every morning. Not much, but it might keep them alive.

Carlito hoped Parvo had been washed out to sea. He peered over the cliff. It was low tide and the sandbar was wide enough for several people to walk to the other island. His eyes moved up to the rocks opposite him. There on a ledge was Parvo, moving carefully as if he'd just woken up and didn't want to fall.

The only reason Carlito didn't start throwing stones at the pirate, for this would be a good way to kill him, was because he saw one of the oars. It was wedged at the high-water mark and, still in one piece, it would make a fine weapon.

He woke Billy and Little Edward. The boys hurried down the steep trail and retrieved the oar, nervous knowing Parvo was watching them. They crept around the northern side of their islet, the oar over Carlito's shoulder as if it were a musket. He limped because of his infected toe and chafed legs.

The tide was low enough that the boys were able to walk through shallow water along the base of the cliff. Caves dotted the rocks like honeycomb. Some went deep into the hillside and echoed loudly with the constant bark of sea lions perched here and there.

In the sixth cave they saw the *tomol*, a small planked Indian canoe. It was turned upside down on a high ledge.

"Let's get it, mateys," shouted Little Edward. He began sloshing toward it in knee-high swells. Suddenly he dropped from sight.

"Edward!"

Carlito and Billy dove after him. Through the clear, green water they could see their friend trying to swim to the surface. He had stepped into a deep hole that extended to the back wall. They pulled him out and crawled back to the mouth of the cave.

Little Edward brushed his dripping hair out of his face. "Think it floats?" he asked.

Carlito's mind raced. If it did float, they might be able to get off the island, but they must hurry. The tide was rising. And Parvo might find them.

28
A Good Plan

Un buen plan

At the back of the cave there were footholds in the rocks. While Little Edward stood guard, the oar a ready weapon should Parvo discover them, Billy and Carlito swam to the ledge and pulled themselves up. The *tomol* easily rolled over and dropped into the water. Whoever had stored the canoe had carefully lashed to it a sturdy paddle carved from driftwood.

Waves swelling into the cave banged the boat against the walls until the boys were able to float it out.

In the sunlight they could see the hull was coated inside and out with asphaltum, the black tar that seeped up from the ocean floor and drifted onto beaches. Carlito's father had used this tar to waterproof their *cayuco*, as well as the roof of their adobe.

"We can't go back the way we came," Carlito decided. "If Parvo sees us he'll beat us up, then he'll try to steal the boat." He remembered the cove Isabella and Maria had found. Even at high tide there was enough beach to keep their canoe from floating away. It would be safe there.

Cautiously the boys climbed in one after the other. Little Edward sat in the middle, both hands clutching the sides, which came up to his shoulders.

Billy took the stern, Carlito the bow. Kneeling, they began to paddle. Gradually they propelled themselves away from the island, far enough so the surf wouldn't push them into the rocks.

As the current was with them, they reached the cove in half an hour, but their legs were damp from a puddle that leaked through the bottom. They pulled the boat high and though it was heavy, managed to lift it onto a flat, dry boulder.

"This will sink before we reach the mainland," said Little Edward, "especially if we try to fit all six of us in it."

Carlito pictured the freshwater streams on Santa Cruz Island, and the mysterious people there who might help them. From the western tip of Anacapa, the island was just four miles away.

"Mates," he said, "I have an idea, but let's talk it over with Billy's father. He'll know what's best."

That afternoon two cannon blasts announced that the *Argentina* and *Santa Rosa* were heading out to open sea. With great relief Carlito and the others watched the sails grow small, then finally disappear into the horizon. To the north they could see the hazy shape of the mainland. Mission San Buenaventura was directly across the channel.

Mr. Bumpus smiled at the boys after Carlito explained his plan. "Good idea, lads, but I'm so sorry. You'll have to do it without me. Billy, my son, you go. These dear lassies will take care of me until help arrives. Go." He had grown so weak he now lay quietly in the sunshine. They all were hungry. And thirsty. The jug was nearly empty.

"What are we waiting for? We could go right now," said Little Edward. "I'm ready. I'll help you paddle, we'll get help and come back tomorrow. Isabella and Maria will take good care of your father, Billy."

Carlito was thinking. There was one problem. Parvo.

If the three boys left the girls alone with Mr. Bumpus, Parvo would come across the sandbar and sneak up here like an old fox. He would cause trouble. As Carlito considered this he realized there was only one way to protect his friends.

29
The New Prisoner
El prisionero nuevo

Parvo was a sorry sight. He'd eaten one live crab that had made him vomit, and he'd had no water in twenty-four hours. His lips were swollen and bloody. As he sat on the sandbar he kept his face down. Billy stood over him with the paddle, and Carlito held the oar.

"One move and we'll smash you," said Little Edward, his arms folded with satisfaction.

Waves sloshed against the *tomol* as Carlito and Billy paddled toward Santa Cruz Island. Parvo sat in the middle, his hands tied behind him with ropes of seaweed. His face was sunburned. When the boys gave him sips of water from an abalone shell, he began to cry.

"More, laddies," he whispered, "please."

"Later," said Carlito, turning forward and storing the jug in front of him. The island looked close enough to touch, but the current and wind seemed to push them backward with every stroke. Their arms ached. They were light-headed from lack of food and their eyes hurt from squinting into the sun.

At least the others are safe, thought Carlito. Isabella and Maria were caring for Mr. Bumpus. Little Edward would help bring food up from the tide pools, and also gather some of the edible plants the girls showed him: prickly pear cactus, sea fig, and sage. They had found pelican and gull nests, but no eggs. The lamb, with its thick wool coat, would provide fresh water each morning — not a lot, but it would help them stay alive.

Before leaving, Carlito had reached in the parrot's cage and stroked his beautiful blue head. "Please eat, Mr. Biscuit. Monty would want you to eat. Be a good boy, please?" One striped eye opened.

"I'll take care of Mr. Biscuit," said Little Edward. "Don't worry."

Mr. Bumpus gathered them for prayer. "Dear Lord, watch over these brave boys. We ask for Your mercy on all of us. Amen."

The waves grew higher with the afternoon wind, and water seeped into the bottom of the *tomol*. Carlito wanted to cry with frustration. Instead of getting closer to the island, they were drifting into the channel. Three porpoises swam alongside as if to encourage him. In the distance an orca leaped above the swells and with a twist of its black-and-white body splashed down. It was swimming behind a pod of whales.

Carlito wished one of these strong animals could tow them ashore. He turned around. Billy looked exhausted. His patch had slipped off and now hung around his neck, and his shirt was soaked from spray.

"Parvo," Carlito said in a hoarse voice, "we need your help. Will you take one of the oars?"

Parvo appeared to be sleeping.

"Mister Parvo!" yelled Carlito. "The sooner you help, the sooner we'll get to fresh water. Please."

When Parvo opened his eyes, there was no longer any hatred. His swollen tongue moved over his lips. "I'll help you," he whispered.

Billy took in his oar and picked up a broken abalone he'd brought as a weapon. He began sawing at the seaweed wrapped around Parvo's wrists.

While Parvo rubbed the circulation back into his fingers, Billy held the sharp-edged shell to the man's neck. Too parched to speak, Billy nicked the skin, drawing blood, which he showed to Parvo.

The pirate nodded, then took up the oar.

30
Justice
Justicia

Parvo was stronger than the boys, but lack of food and water and sleep had weakened him. When he realized the swells had carried the *tomol* into the channel, far away from both islands, he lay the paddle across his lap.

"I am sorry, Spaniard."

Carlito said nothing. He uncorked the jug, took a sip, then passed it to Parvo. To Carlito's surprise, the pirate offered it first to Billy, and not until the boy had taken a swig, did he have one himself.

Carlito woke to a terrible headache. The sun glared off the waves like a mirror. He was so thirsty his mouth hung open. Billy and Parvo lay in the boat's watery bottom.

A flock of white birds flew swiftly toward them and a voice shouted, *"¡Hola!"* Carlito blinked. Everything looked blurry, but when the voice again called out he saw that, instead of birds, he was seeing sails on a large ship, a schooner. And there were men staring down at him.

He felt himself being carried over someone's shoulder then rolled onto the hard deck. A cup was pressed to his lips. Water ran down his chin and into his mouth. He swallowed. How good it tasted.

Was that Papá smiling at him?

"Carlito . . . Carlito, can you hear me? It's your uncle . . . thank God we've found you."

"Tío Roberto?"

"Sí, m'ijo." He held Carlito in his strong arms. "I've been searching for you everywhere. When Ziba told us what happened, we came after *la fragata negra*, but always a day too late, unfortunately. Thank God your tiny boat floated into the channel or we would not have found you in time."

Tío Roberto looked so much like Papá, his brother. He lifted Carlito and started to carry him down the companionway, to a berth.

"No, tío, please, my friends . . ."

"Your friends are being cared for, don't worry."

But when Carlito told him about Mr. Bumpus and the others, and about Montague, tío Roberto walked to the stern, shouting orders.

The schooner pitched and rolled in the swells as it changed direction, heading into the wind for Anacapa. High from the mizzenmast flew the flag of Spain. Storm clouds were beginning to darken the sky, however.

Carlito sat on deck, leaning against a barrel by the foremast, the cold wind stinging his face. The shadow of Anacapa Island was growing nearer. With sadness he watched the rising, foaming sea. He knew they would need to wait out the storm, anchored in one of the sheltered coves. It might be days before the ship could sail back into the channel and many more days before they'd reach Montague. The thought of her perishing from thirst horrified Carlito. He bowed his head.

Billy came to sit next to him. He nodded toward Parvo, who was being questioned by tío Roberto and three men in uniform. "Now's our chance for revenge, Spaniard. Say the word and together we will cut his throat, then throw him overboard like Montague did to Red Cap. We can do it fast, before anyone stops us."

"Yes, *amigo*, we could do that. But I am tired. And I am especially tired of hating Parvo."

"I'm not."

"Billy, your father is right. This pirate needs to be brought to justice for his terrible crimes. That is something Governor Solá can do. As for me, when I get home I want to ride my horse. I want to talk to my mother and I want to taste her delicious *gazpacho*."

Billy tilted his head to squint out of his good eye. "I still think we should kill him."

"Let's talk about it tomorrow, *amigo*. Look, there." Carlito pointed to the island. Running high along the bluff was Little Edward, jumping and waving his white shirt. As two boats were lowered and rowed to the sandbar, Carlito glanced again at Parvo. His hands were tied behind his back and soldiers were leading him down into the hold.

Carlito turned away. He watched the island where a small procession of sailors climbed up the cliff to help his friends.

Epilogue

Epílogo

After raiding Alta California the *Argentina* and *Santa Rosa* continued south. They anchored off the island of Ceres (*"Isla de Cerros"*) in Baja California. For nearly one month they hunted sea lions, elephant seals, and deer, made repairs aboard ship, then stored water and firewood.

According to Captain Corney, on January 24, 1819, they captured and sank a merchant brig near Cabo San Lucas. Days later a shore party landed at Islas Tres Marias for wood and water, and found a root similar to the taro plant of the Sandwich Islands. It unfortunately turned out to be poison and twelve Sandwich Islanders from Bouchard's crew suffered agonizing deaths.

They sailed past the Galápagos Islands, then on July 9, 1819, the *Santa Rosa* anchored at Valparaiso, Chile. Eight days later the *Argentina* arrived in desperate need of food and water: Forty more of Bouchard's men had died.

Captain Corney asked Bouchard for his pay and share of booty, telling the Frenchman he was disgusted with pirating and planned to return to England on the first brig out. But Bouchard refused. Corney would be paid only if he continued the voyage with him, south around Cape Horn and up to Buenos Aires. Infuriated, Corney left the *Santa Rosa* in charge of his first lieutenant, Mr. Woodburn, and found berth on another ship. He arrived in London several months later.

Peter Corney died in 1836 while sailing to British Columbia, where he was to begin a prestigious job with Hudson's Bay Company. It is said his widow and children settled in Honolulu.

Eventually Bouchard served as commander in chief with the Peruvian navy and was rewarded with a spice and cocoa plantation. The old pirate treated his slaves with such cruelty, however, they staged a revolt in 1837 and killed him.

In 1910 a breakwater was constructed in southern California off San Pedro and Wilmington, which later enclosed Long Beach, too. Treasure hunters could walk along the jagged rocks from Terminal Island to Dead Man's Island where artifacts were dug up, including many graves. In 1927 three graves set off from the others revealed two males with conquistador boots, an old sword, and a female skeleton with long blond tresses. Months later dredgers began scooping away the little island in order to widen the harbor of San Pedro, today one of the safest seaports in the world.

Epilogue

The two Indian girls who were taken from San Juan Capistrano were probably from the Juaneño Band of Mission Indians, or the Acjachemen people as they originally called themselves. Scholars estimate that when Spaniards built the mission in 1776 there were several hundred thousand Juaneños living along the beaches and hillsides of southern California.

Though Anacapa Island has no fresh water, sheep periodically were raised there. During the night their wool absorbed so much dew that by morning they were wet as sponges. The sheep "drank" simply by licking each other.

Glossary

Glosario

[*Sp.*: Spanish]

abalone—sea mollusk in an oval shell perforated near the edge, lined with mother-of-pearl
adobe—a building made from bricks of sun-dried clay
aft—toward the rear, or stern, of a ship
aguardiente—[*Sp.*] fiery alcoholic drink
amigo—[*Sp.*] friend
barkentine—a sailing vessel with its two forward masts square-rigged and its rear mast rigged fore and aft
belaying pins—removable wooden pins in a ship's rail around which rope can be wrapped
bicorn hat—crescent-shaped hat with two "corners"
bodega—[*Sp.*] wine cellar
bo's'n—[boatswain] a ship's officer in charge of the deck crew, anchors, rigging
bow—the front part of a ship
bowsprit—a large, tapered spar extending forward from the bow of a sailing vessel

rig—1.) a two-masted ship with square sails 2.) the jail aboard a warship

bullock—a young or castrated bull; used especially for meat and hide

capstan—huge winch for hauling in the anchor

carreta—[*Sp.*] long, narrow cart

cayuco—[Spanish-American] small fishing boat

Chumash—Indian tribe from central and southern California

churros—[*Sp.*] fried strips of dough, often rolled in sugar

companionway—a staircase between a ship's decks

corvette—a sailing warship, larger than a sloop, smaller than a frigate, usually with one row of cannons

Costanoan—Indian tribe from northern California

cutter—a small boat that can cut swiftly through the water, carried aboard larger ships

El Camino Real—[*Sp.*] the Royal Highway, now California's Highway 101

Esselen—coastal Indian tribe, north central California; their hot springs are now privately owned by the Esalen Institute

fandango—[*Sp.*] a lively Spanish dance

forecastle—[fo'c's'le] upper deck of a ship in front of the foremast; sailors' quarters at the front of the ship

fragata negra—[*Sp.*] black frigate

frigate—a fast, medium-sized sailing warship from the 18th and early 19th centuries, usually carrying between 24 to 60 cannons

Gabrieleños—Indian tribe from southern California
gaitas—[*Sp.*] Spanish bagpipes
galley—a ship's kitchen
garibaldi—a bright orange-colored fish found off southern California's Channel Islands
gaviota—[*Sp.*] seagull
gig—a long, light ship's boat used by the commanding officer
goleta—[*Sp.*] schooner
gracias—[*Sp.*] thank you
halyard—rope or tackle for raising or lowering a sail or flag
hawsehole—holes in the ship's bow through which the anchor cable or a hawser is passed
head—the front part of a ship; bow; ship's lavatory
hijo, hija—[*Sp.*] son, daughter [*m'ijo* = my son]; term of affection
hoosegow—jail [corruption of Spanish word *juzgado*]
hold—very bottom of a ship
insubordination—not submitting to authority
jib—the triangular sail in front of the foremast
launch—the largest boat carried by a warship
manta ray—a large fish with a horizontal, flat body, winglike fins, and a long, thin tail
mariposa—[*Sp.*] butterfly
mission—a church built by Spaniards who wanted to bring Christianity to the California Indians. There were 21 in all, a chain of them that ran for nearly 600 miles along the Royal Highway, from San Diego Alcalá

(1769) to San Francisco Solano (1823).

mizzenmast—the mast closest to the stern of a ship in a vessel with two or more masts

orca—a large, black-and-white dolphin that eats other mammals and fish with its teeth

pinnace—a ship's small sailing boat

pirata—[*Sp.*] pirate

poop deck—highest deck at the back of a ship

port—the left side of a ship

powder monkeys—young boys who delivered fresh gunpowder to the cannons

presidio—a military post or fort

pueblo—a communal village, usually made of flat-roofed abobes

quarterdeck—at stern of ship, usually reserved for officers

rancho—[*Sp.*] ranch

scurvy—disease affecting sailors on long voyages; lack of vitamin C caused loss of teeth, internal bleeding, exhaustion and dizziness; often resulted in death. Eating onions, potatoes, or citrus fruit, such as limes, will cure it; British sailors were thus called "limeys"

sea cucumber—soft, leathery echinoderm, lives buried under tidal rocks or sand

sea fig—iceplant with purple flower; its fruit is edible

señor, señora—[*Sp.*] Mr., Mrs.

sextant—instrument used by navigators to measure the distance of the sun, stars, etc., from the horizon to determine a ship's position

shanghaied—to be captured and forced to work on a ship. This term comes from the time when sailors were kidnapped for voyages to and from Shanghai, China

sí—[*Sp.*] yes

siesta—[*Sp.*] a nap or rest taken after the noon meal

sombrero—[*Sp.*] hat

starboard—the right side of a ship

stern—rear end of a ship

tiburón—[*Sp.*] shark

Timoteo—[*Sp.*] Timothy

tinderbox—a metal box to hold tinder and flint for starting a fire; also to hold burning coals

tío, tía—[*Sp.*] uncle, aunt

tomol—[Chumash] planked canoe used by the Chumash to travel along the coast and offshore islands

wardroom quarter gallery—captain's lavatory

yawl—small sailboat with two masts: a tall one near the center, and a short one near the stern

zapatos—[*Sp.*] shoes

Bibliography

Bibliografía

Batman, Richard. *The Outer Coast.* San Diego: Harcourt Brace Jovanovich, 1985.

Bealer, Lewis W. "Bouchard in the Islands of the Pacific." *The Pacific Historical Review*, Vol. IV, No. 4 (December, 1935), pp. 328–342.

Botting, Douglas. *The Pirates.* Alexandria, VA: Time-Life Books, 1978.

Busch, Briton Cooper, ed. *Alta California 1840–1842: The Journal and Observations of William Dane Phelps, Master of the Ship "Alert."* Glendale, CA: The Arthur H. Clark Co., 1983.

Caire, Helen. *Santa Cruz Island: A History and Recollections of an Old California Rancho.* Spokane, WA: The Arthur H. Clark Co., 1993.

California Coastal Access Guide. Berkeley, CA: University of California Press, 1981.

Caughey, John and Laree, eds. *California Heritage.* Itasca, IL: F. E. Peacock Publishers, 1975.

Corney, Peter. *Early Northern Pacific Voyages.* Honolulu: Thomas G. Thrum, Publisher, 1896.

Dana, Richard Henry. *Two Years Before the Mast.* London: Everyman's Library, 1912.

Dos Californios. Santa Barbara, CA: Bellerophon Books, 1978.

Gerhard, Peter. *Pirates of the Pacific, 1575–1742.* Lincoln, NE: University of Nebraska Press, 1990.

Gleason, Duncan. *The Islands and Ports of California.* New York: Devin-Adaire Co., 1958.

Granberry, Michael. "A Tribe's Battle for Its Identity." *Los Angeles Times* (March 13, 1994), pp. A1, 22.

Grupe, Henry E. *The Frigates.* Alexandria, VA: Time-Life Books, 1979.

Heizer, Robert F., ed. *Handbook of North American Indians: California*, Vol. VIII. Washington, DC: Smithsonian Institute, 1978.

Hunt, Rockwell Dennis. *Oxcart to Airplane.* Los Angeles: Powell Publishing Co., 1929.

Judd, Bernice. *Voyages to Hawaii Before 1860.* Honolulu: The University Press of Hawaii, 1974.

Lucie-Smith, Edward. *Outcasts of the Sea: Pirates and Piracy.* Norwalk, CT: The Eaton Press, 1978.

Morison, Samuel Eliot. *Old Bruin: Commodore Matthew Calbraith Perry.* Norwalk, CT: The Eaton Press, 1967.

Murphy, Bill. *A Pictorial History of California.* San Francisco: Fearon Publishers, 1958.

O'Dell, Scott. *Country of the Sun.* New York: Crowell, 1957.

Parry, J. H. *Romance of the Sea.* Washington, DC: National Geographic Society, 1981.

Platt, Richard; illustrated by Stephen Biesty. *Cross-Sections Man-of-War.* London: Dorling Kindersley, 1993.

Reinstedt, Randall A. *Tales, Treasures and Pirates of Old Monterey.* Carmel, CA: Ghost Town Publications, 1976.

Riegel, Martin P. *A Ship Lover's Guide to California.* San Clemente, CA: Riegel Publishing, 1988.

Robinson, W.W. *Los Angeles, From the Days of the Pueblo.* San Francisco: California Historical Society, 1981.

Rolle, Andrew F. *California: A History.* New York: Thomas Y. Crowell, 1969.

Roske, Ralph J. *Everyman's Eden: A History of California.* New York: Macmillan, 1968.

Stegner, Page; photographs by Frans Lanting. *Islands of the West.* San Francisco: Sierra Club Books, 1985.

Walker, Doris. *Home Port for Romance.* Dana Point, CA: To-the-Point Press, 1981.

Whelan, Nicholas. *Anacapa.* Globe, AZ: Southwest Parks and Monuments Assoc. trail booklet, no date.

Wilbur, C. Keith, M.D. *Pirates and Patriots of the Revolution.* Old Saybrook, CT: The Globe Pequot Press, 1984.

Wilbur, C. Keith, M.D. *Revolutionary Medicine: 1700–1800.* Old Saybrook, CT: The Globe Pequot Press, 1980.

Wilson, Florence Slocum. *Windows on Early California.* Los Angeles: The National Society of the Colonial Dames of America, 1971.

Young, Stanley; photographs by Melba Levick. *The Missions of California.* San Francisco: Chronicle Books, 1988.